# Half & Half

## *Short Stories*

IN ENGLISH & SPANISH

*Short Stories*

IN ENGLISH & SPANISH

HELENA PANEYKO

*published by*

THE VOICE OF SPANISH

HALF & HALF
Short Stories



Printed in the United States of America



PUBLISHED BY
The Voice of Spanish
Port Townsend, Washington

ISBN 978-1537756226

Library of Congress Control Number: 2016916985
CreateSpace Independent Publishing Platform, North Charleston, SC

Cover Photo by Marina Puszyn

Book Design by Ruth Marcus

Text is set in Minion

## *Introduction and Dedication*

So many things in life happen by chance...others happen because we planned them.

The writing of this book has a little bit of both but at different stages. Started by change, doing some writing from my heart as a way to let out what I was thinking and feeling. Inspirations keep coming, even if I was not looking for them, sometimes as the water flowing non-stop on a river, sometimes calm, others wildly. Daydreaming or in my real night dreams, a conversation, a picture, an animal, a drop of rain, a phrase I have read or heard somewhere became an urgent call to write. The stories kept piling up and I started collecting them.

One day, the site I was using disappeared. It got hacked along with my email. I panicked, of course. Then, I realized how important it was to recall the ones I could and do something with them. I wanted to share my inspirations and my experiences. I also wanted to go that extra step to show that, in spite of all the difficulties and challenges, which I now call "opportunities", I could make it happened.

I know that my second language, English, in which half of the book is written, might have some "interesting twists".

You have now in your hands an open book, literally and figuratively. Vulnerable, I am. Proud as well.

I want to thank all who had crossed their paths with mine; from my extraordinary parents Pierre and Eugenia, my three sisters María, María Eugenia and Jacqueline, my children Alejandro y Daniela, my daughter-in-law Aurélie, my grandbebita Amelia, my extended family, my special friends, acquaintances, my professors, classmates, co-workers and students, my cat Lady Gata helping me with the keyboard now sitting on my shoulder, animals and flowers, a warm smile at a bus station. All of you have made me who I am today. Special thanks, and I know I am going to forget to name some people (I apologize in advance), to all that had believed in me, to Richard Auler, Robin White, Marina Puszyn, Madeline McClure, Karli Mueller, Glenn Acevedo, Claire and George Alkire, Loly Lopez, Luzarelys Gomez, Marina LaGrave, Leonard and Gitte Zweig, the Koval family, Fiona Daly, Ursula Ahrens, Ruth Marcus and many, many more.

A beautiful life is everywhere.

# *Table of Contents*

**HISTORIAS CORTAS EN ESPANOL (SHORT STORIES IN SPANISH)**

Half&Half: Short Stories

# *Foreword / Prólogo*

Our pilgrimage through this life draws us all into contact with fascinating events and personalities. A delightful rarity is Helena Paneyko, whom we first met some fifteen years ago as neighbors on a rural island in Puget Sound, Washington.

An intrepid international traveler, successful immigrant-now-citizen, eternal optimist, lover of nature and life, multi-lingual profesora, Airbnb hostess, fellow Believer, thoughtful people watcher, mother of two successful children, inspired writer—Helena is all these. And we have been blessed with a friendship that has extended over the years into ongoing conversations about life's camino encanto.

Thankfully, Helena now has collected stories of her heart into book form. And so, amigos, con mucho gusto we invite you to pour your favorite cup of tea and commune comfortably here with creative Helena. May you find blessings in her company, as do we.

GEORGE and CLAIRE ALKIRE
Sequim, Washington

# *English Stories*

# *CAMINO DE SANTIAGO*
## *(ONE WOMAN'S PERSONAL JOURNEY)*

Many years ago I had the opportunity to read a book by Paulo Coelho entitled 'The Pilgrimage (The Diary of a Magus)'. The book tells the story of a journey along the route of Santiago de Compostela, but more importantly, it shares the journey of self-discovery.

This book cast a magic spell over my life, and it is only fitting that I retraced some of the steps of Coelho in real life, as I had in my dreams. The idea of doing so became a silent obsession, and finally the day came when I began my own Camino, a journey without expectations. My motives? I didn't know at the time, only that I had to do it. I decided to begin my adventure in Lisbon, Portugal. With my two walking sticks and my backpack filled with what I thought were the 'essentials', I began to walk. The 'essentials' became a heavy and unnecessary burden. Half of them were soon left behind, the first of many lessons.

My Camino was 256 kilometers (about 160 miles) long. Much of it traced a route that is both a European Cultural Route and a World Heritage site. As I ambled along, I could not escape the feeling that I had crept into a fairy tale, meeting a panoply of characters, young and old, both wise and naive. Each one of them shared what I needed to receive at that time: their own stories, their humble lives, their homes and what scant possessions they had, without hesitation. Each episode, each hostel, each tired and sore footstep was repaid in epiphany and self-knowledge. My confidence increased, and I learned to trust my instincts again. Maps and location of the refugios in this fairy world often do not align with the maps of the real world. They showed instead the length between points of respite, and acted as nonexistent phantoms on my long trip.

But every *cafecito*, each *buen camino* from other pilgrims or locals felt like winning the lottery. I am the winner! At the end, when I arrived in Santiago de Compostela and celebrated my accomplishment, I felt such richness that I had to share my newfound wealth of wisdom.

Now I find myself back in Port Townsend, after a ten years' absence during which I had the opportunity to study, learn new skills and travel the world. What travel! From tennis in Texas to beautiful organic farms in Ireland. California, Spain, Portugal, Germany, all so different, so challenging, all with their own appeal and secrets to be ferreted out. Each wonderful in their own way. With my feet back on the familiar ground of Port Townsend, my transition years have turned into transmission years. Happy to be back, happy wherever I go!

## *Dedicated to You*

I am learning to love myself without regret,
and someone waits for me just beyond reach,
his arms open, heart beating in unison, in a choir
echoed in the space between our embrace.
It is our present, our future, fulfilled in dreams,
in hope, in open minds. We have both been waiting
for this moment to arrive,
we have prepared the soil without knowing why.
Now the answer is clear, no doubts are in our minds,
soon we will walk together, holding hands,
along the new road of our lives.

# *Light*

Today at 4 p.m., I entered the library. The first two letters of 'library' are the same as the first two letters of 'light'. Light provided to the community, through words, through readings and research, through communication. Light from the bulbs, lightweight, lighting the candles when there is no energy or when the time is sacred, light from the heart and from the soul.

For many years I walked in darkness, in the shadows of the modern world, hiding from abuse, from bullying, even from my closest family. Step by step, looking around, seeing what I was not allowed to observe, hearing when I was not permitted to listen, like a little chicken. I started picking on that cage that was intended for my protection. I knew there was something more, something missing. I could feel the other colors, smells, the different sounds.

One day, I went to the forest with my dog Moss. He was my best friend, my only friend. He looked to me with his big, brown eyes which seemed to ask, perplexed, "where are we going?" I had no idea at that time, I only knew that we had to go. So we began to walk, and we walked for a very long time until we came upon a rock. I sat down, and Moss beside me. I began to talk aloud to this listener who could not respond with my language. I felt safe. I let out all the stories which I could remember from my childhood.

He listened as if he could understand. In a way, it was like writing in the sand, talking into the wind, where the words disappear into the sky and the sea.

Suddenly I heard a voice, clear and strong. It was my inner voice responding. It began to tell me of a bigger and wider world, it was lighting my path, not pushing me away from my past.

'Why not, why not?' I kept repeating to myself as Moss wagged his tail in approval of our upcoming journey. I wanted to learn the boundaries of my own resources. I wanted to know myself, to know that I was made of good wood that had seasoned in hard weather. The tears and sorrow had not saturated the wood with their salty moisture; I was convinced of my value and beauty.

We walked without a destination and with an open mind. I knew we were doing the right thing, and yet I was also aware of danger. I remembered that nothing could have been worse than what I experienced at home. I was also aware of the challenges and the risks I was taking, but what would have happened if I had never left?

We passed villages and towns, small and big cities I could have only imagined through my books, which had been my hidden escape and to which I owed all previous knowledge of the world. But now I could see it all with my own eyes! Everything I read of was real, and there I was a character in my own bold story. Moss, a well-trained puppy, and I were welcomed into homes and shelters, under some bridges and into decadent mansions. Everyone wanted to know our endless story, to spoil us with kindness. Perhaps we were a kind of inspiration to some, an opportunity to shine for others.

I remember one homeless man in particular. His name was Barry. He had long hair and a long beard. He was also on a unique journey. He was gentle with his words and wise in his advice. He told us about his younger days, when he 'won the lottery' by going to war. "I was so immature," he said, "and I even enjoyed playing with the weapons, building muscles to look like Popeye, smoking for the first time, getting drunk, 'serving my country'. I also had a dog, Rita. I never saw her again..." He grew silent as his eyes welled with tears. The three of us shared a dinner under the street lights of Portugal. How did we end up there? Destiny?

The night turned into day. The sun came, smiling, inviting us to continue our journey. We had no plan, no written schedule. After some hours Moss grew tired, and we walked slower and took in spring's new flowers, a cool breeze softly stroking our faces. We found a river and decided to take a siesta. I had no idea what time it was, but the moon peeked its round face above the trees, smiling a protection upon us. We feel asleep there, were a woman, as a fairy godmother, came to our riverside bed.

"My child," she said, "you are a brave girl. Where do you belong?"

"I belong to the world," I replied, "I belong to the Universe. I am part of everything and everyone, and everything and everyone are a part of me." She grew lighter and I continued, "Can I change how the fish swim, can I modify the birds' flight, stop the trees from flowering, the whales from singing, the rain from falling?"

"You do not need to change a thing," the fairy godmother chuckled, "the order and creation of the world is perfect, the harmony between all creatures and the

Universe is superb. Continue your growth and share your message throughout the world. Let the rivers flow, let the plants nurture you, let the bees do their job. Enjoy every sound, every smell, every hug. Life is a blessing as are you." And with that, she disappeared.

With renewed energy we continued our odyssey. We climbed mountains, crossed plains and jungles, saw people from such different cultures but who, in the end, were all the same human with different flesh and bones, with distinct opportunities. Some, like me, will take the challenges upon themselves, while others will stay where they belong.

The seasons have followed, and now my hair is covered in silver threads, nearly white, and my fingers are crooked. My skin bearing the scars of time that no longer hurt me. But my journey has not ended, I am still alive.

I belong to life, to the circle of life.

# *Spring*

Flowers are reborn with fresh fragrance and bright colors
they will nurture birds and bees.

Bears awaken from their slumber
they will meet a world again.

Earth is ready and clean following hard snow and rain.
New hopes and dreams come along with a new season
to brighten up our lives and fill them with loving care.

The sound of nature is music to my ears,
Makes my soul dance, makes my spirit beat
with the rhythm of the wind, from dusk
till dawn, from night until day.

# *Butterflies*

Once upon a time, a fly got stuck while feasting on a stich of butter. Not being able to spread its wings, as they were covered in the yellow and creamy substance, she expected her end to be near and decided to enjoy the sweet delicacy with her last sigh before falling asleep.

When she awoke, her wings had changed color and appeared to be giant in comparison to the original boring, blackish-translucent ones she'd had before. More importantly, the fly could actually fly again. She called upon her sisters and brothers, who at first did not recognize her as she had changed so much.

However, telling her story made the other flies want to look as colorful, and so the butter was quickly covered in flies expecting their magical transformation. Soon after, butterflies of many colors and shapes emerged from the mix.

This is the story of how the butterflies' journey came into being.

While the multi-colored creatures enjoyed their new looks, they were still curious as to why this had happened to them. There must have been a reason, and so they called a meeting. There they discussed their newfound metamorphosis and came to an important realization: they were on a mission, and the mission was simple: Go and spread. Not the butter, but a message of peace, of joy, and of enlightenment. Go and pollinate like the bees, go and fly in swarms around the world, go and compete for survival after crossing continents and oceans.

So they went, and found that all was well and fine as it is in an ideal world. People referred to having butterflies in their tummies when describing a certain state of excitement. Flowers opened their petals, welcoming the sweet caress of the butterflies' tongues and their stories of travels and encounters with other relatives.

One day, an urgent message was relayed around the globe. All butterflies were called to a very important conclave where an old giant tree grew, a tree which was considered very wise because of his age and experiences. He had for millennia served his flying friends while they were migrating. He had provided shelter and food for them. But now something had changed: the tree was missing his lepidoptera. They were not coming anymore and he was concerned, and he worried about the new situation, as were his brethren.

When the convention began there were many speakers and all of them felt troubled. They could not understand why all these changes were happening. Then a beautiful butterfly took the stand and said in a very somber tone, "We are dying. Our finishing line has moved closer and has shortened our lifespan. Many species are already extinct. We cannot do much ourselves. We need help. Humans have to realize that when we are gone, they will be next in line.

"As long as pollution continues, as long as industries are careless, as long as farmers are spraying with insecticides, they will be fighting a battle against nature, a battle they will never win.

"It's time humans start caring for each other, and for the planet and everything on it. It's not too late for change, there is still a small window of opportunity," advised the beautiful butterfly.

"Let us send out our cry to the world, someone might hear us!"

## *Soul Prints*

Let the pen kiss the paper,
entering the soul,
swimming in blood
with the narcotic desire
to share memories,
to build dreams,
to escape to freedom.

Experiences tattoed my heart
with drawings of love, birth,
growth, joy, passion and pain.
My voice sounds in the silence
of the written words,
while my light guides me
to a different world.

# *Fog*

It's quite foggy this morning. I'm up at the crack of dawn, there is a mysterious feeling about the day to come, but difficult to see clearly at this time. Milagro, the red-haired calf, is already calling to me, her stand-in mom. She roars innocently, already recognizing me from a distance. It is the blue bucket which she's after. I call her name and she is wagging her tail in anticipation of a good meal, sweet words and a gentle touch

The ghostly murk spans across the field, confusing my path. Holding onto my stick (one never goes near cattle without one, I'm told), I steadily cross toward the cows and calves roaming in the fog. I'm so content I begin to sing aloud, a favorite song from my childhood: "Si mi querencia es el monte" by Simon Diaz. The animals don't care if I'm out of tune. I sound like one of them, anyway!

Singing in tune is not one of my fortes, I must admit, but my new audience is very forgiving. Maybe they are deaf. Today, all the cows and calves are doing well, and I continue along the hedges, admiring the presents which nature so generously gives us daily. I stopped to watch the dew on the tips of the branches, perfect drops not yet ready to fall. They hang from spider webs, knitted with patience and precision. To move my fingers freely, I take off my gloves and ask, is it time to learn a new skill which will help when age has affected my joints?

Inspired in so many ways, I can still learn! The dense fog begins to thin…

# *Immortal*

The cat is curled on the windowsill, watching the wind and rain bashing the leafless trees. Threatening dark clouds hang low today, making it impossible for even the smallest of sunrays to reach the earth. Another dull day passes, grey and cold, while nature is washing away the dust, preparing for a new cycle of growth.

It is nearly dinner time and finally the sun makes its last attempt to break through the clouds, unsuccessfully I might add. The moon peeps over the distant mountains, a pale crescent, ready to make his way through the dark sky.

Some stars arrive with the moon, slowly, as if waiting for the sun to completely disappear. Since time began the stars have taken their positions every night, as if suspended in the air by some invisible thread covering the sky. Those stars are guiding us when there is no light, they help us in ways similar to the caring guidance that our mothers gave us. Many years ago, after my mother boarded her last trip, I felt comfortable thinking that she was now the brightest star in the sky, watching down on us, sending us her love. She will always be present in our lives, not only when I'm looking into the night sky illuminated by all those stars.

*Mañana* (tomorrow) will be another day, and the sun will appear a little earlier. She seems lazy these days, hardly visible, as if hibernating beneath her blanket of fog, waiting for the new energies of spring to take over and begin the eternal routine of annual seasons yet again.

The feline turns around, jumping into my lap and massaging my leg with her claws. She does this as if making bread, purring with a soft sound, feeling loved.

# *Calling Beaks*

I stand before my glass window, watching day after day as much as I can. I watch with the naive curiosity of a child I do not want to lose, impatient to see the day progress, for something which will call my attention.

Two birds arrive everyday with all kinds of debris in their beaks, knitting a nest with precision and care. They come and go, diligent in their mission: to build a home, a unique home for their family.

More than a week passes and I observe a few changes. At first, they stop flying as much as before. They seem to be quietly resting, cozy and warm. Once in a while, they go for a fly and then quickly return. The nest is high, so high that I can only imagine what is happening inside.

Another week, ten days pass, and again another change in their routine. I must look for some rocks to stand on, but when I find them, I lose my balance. I feel as if I'm a novice trapeze artist, but I  really want to see what is going on!

Five small eggs, beige and bespeckled, wait their turns to hatch. They seem to shake ever so slightly. I do not want to touch them. I do not want to disturb nature.

Another day passes, and five creatures, naked, half-ugly, come to life. They already have the energy to open their beaks and call to their parents, requesting food and kisses. The parents have no time to rest, coming and going, again and again, in order to feed these babies.

Tuesday, baby #1 decides he is big enough to try his first flight. He stands at the edge of the nest: 'Here I am, here I go!' he seems to say. He spreads his tiny, trembling wings, and jumps.

Alas, his first attempt fails and now he is on the ground, looking lost and calling mom. The second sibling, not wanting to be any less brave, follows suit. Eventually, all five of them end up on the ground.

They stay close together, exploring their new world. Mom and dad come around a few times to feed them but then they leave. The five are left to survive, to go on with their own lives.

It is a tough love, but such is life. It is the way it was designed to be, for them and for us. My nest is empty, my children have spread their trembling wings and flown. I have to allow them to live their lives, to let them go. Like birds, they have learned how to stand up when they fall. I have observed them from a distance, watching them fly high, spreading their wings with confidence. The time has come when they too will build their own nests. I am a proud mom!

## *The Tree and The Monkey*

I recently read a story about a tree and a monkey that made me stop and think.

The tree is planted, with roots holding it safely, as if it is screwed into the earth, with strong branches opening up like arms to the sky. The wind goes gently through his leaves, and once in awhile a heavy storm challenges the tree's ability to stand straight. The rain soaks the earth where he stands, and the sun gives him the energy to grow fruits and flowers, either for us or the wildlife around him. He grows stronger as the years go by, lending support for a hammock on sunny days and shade to the passers-by. But all together it is a quiet and boring existence.

In stark contrast, a monkey jumps around a lot. He enjoys life all the time, swinging from branch to branch, tasting different fruits, smelling flowers, going up and down nearly all the time. Occasionally he slows down but not for long. With renewed energy and enthusiasm, he starts up again.

"Sometimes, I would love to be the monkey, but I am attached to the ground", said the tree.

"Sometimes, I would love to have roots like you, but then I would have to slow down, but I love my mobility and do not want to slow down" responded the monkey. They then discussed their differences in detail, and as neither had a choice they decided to celebrate their differences and cheered for all the blessings they were gifted.

While both the tree and the monkey lived very different lives, their existence is part of the great circle of life. A tree will always be a tree, and a monkey will always be a monkey! One question remains: do I want to be a tree or a monkey, or rather, will I follow my mind or my heart?

# *Legacy*

Can we plan for it, or does it simply happen on its own?
Must we wait until we are dead, or can we embody
our legacy as we walk through this world?
These are questions I have asked myself
before receiving this surprising comment,
"I have already left a great legacy in someone's life."
I felt honored and humbled
by those words which answered my curiosity,
and simply said thank you in a very honest way
to this person who was able to speak my truth,
who had already left a great legacy in my life,
a living and special one, which I will always retain.

# *Tears*

The grey and black bird walks on a grass damp from rain which fell just moments before. She runs with her beak full of sticks, ready for the construction of her nest. A few smaller birds pick at the bread crumbs that I have just thrown into the yard. They Sunday-feast before my eyes, serenading in return as if thanking me.

I am thinking about the great melodies of nature, unheard when you do not have the time or when your ears are plugged with tiny, plastic speakers, the music preselected and heard before.

To reach for the unknown is scary at times, to see the invisible winds die, to hear the silence curled around a language so private and unique it cannot be multiplied. The words from Anton Corbijn now come to mind, "A man with everything in the world looking for a quiet place to sit…" and they make me want to cry. My tears are of joy, different from those of pain. The emotions embodied in them carry distinct substances, different chemicals inside.

What is it that they hold within? Are they hiding real sorrow, dishonest, pretending to act otherwise? As someone once said, tears are emotion's perspiration, the sweat of our hearts.

Those who have survived a war seem to be hardened by it. They have cried over their myriad losses. Crying is justified in different ways, perhaps some tears are more profound than others.

Some cultures allow crying, while others reserve it for one gender of society despite the lyrics, 'Big girls don't cry…'. At the end I can only say, it is okay to cry.

## *Whispers*

Whispering raindrops falling
gently to the ground
their wet magic
touch refreshing the earth
nurturing the rivers, lakes
and our souls.
The acid one burns the soil
I can sense it on my skin
the thunder louder than the drilling rig
painfully cracking the surface
and the earthquake trembles under my feet.

Whispering tears from the trees
landing softly,
as clear as morning dew,
they look like crystals landing
melting under the rising sun
and their softness wakens the leaves.

Whispering sounds from the wind
sometimes loud, sometimes
not, as thunder roars deep in my ears.

Whispering music from the sea
waves hitting the rocks
bringing floating plastic and poisoned dead fish
as a reminder
of our carelessness
that is responsible for the suffering of many creatures.
Rage sets in as I succumb to this helplessness.
Fury tsunami washes my skin.

Whispering melodies from tribal drums
traditions passed on to those who follow
imploring, begging for support. Their wisdom
is timeless. But who is listening?

Whispering flames from the fire
warming our feet as we walk the path
of our journey driven by consciousness—or is it
destiny which guides us? A volcano exploded
which sent ashes all over,
scripting S.O.S. in ashes across the sky
but who reads them?

Whispering songs from nature
a mixture
of happiness and sorrow,
crying, shouting:
"I WILL SURVIVE'.

# *Seventeen Minutes, and More Shades of Grey and Green*

Seventeen more minutes to go…the washing machine was nearly finished yesterday when my Skype phone rang. God bless modern technology; I can 'talk' to my 8-month old granddaughter while she's in a park with her dad, and much more importantly, I can see her through the screen of my cell phone. On this day, she was filling her mouth with air and then pushing her bulging cheeks in to let the air out in funny sounds that made me laugh. She will soon learn how to blow out the candles on her birthday cakes.

Suddenly, I looked up into the sky and realized how different it is here compared to the places I have lived. But that day, and only for a few moments, I recognized a strange shape up there, a cloud that did not last long but for whose fleeting moment possessed the figure of a friendly dragon. Its shape was surrounded by many shades of grey. Clouds laden with rain. The timid rays of the sun barely drew the silhouette, and then in a flash, it was gone.

It reminded me of the days when we were in a nearly-cloudless place in the Caribbean, where the occasional cloud threw our young imaginations into full swing and ignited complex stories around the short-lived images.

But here in Ireland, where I now live, most of the time I only get to count the shades of grey and green. The darkest clouds seem to carry the most rain and when they open, the heavy drops sound as if someone was drumming on the roof. Looking out the window, I can see the first drops falling again and can almost feel the plants enjoying a refreshing shower. Why a garden hose exist here, I do not know; the rain transforms the very life it touches.

Just as the clouds relieve themselves of the burden of their weight, so I let go of my worries. Holding onto them won't change anything, I tell myself as I watch the raindrops slide the accumulated dirt off of my window, sometimes with a gentle touch though more often with clamoring force.

When the rain is over and the sun comes out again, the multiple green shades of the leaves look as if someone had spent a long time polishing them. The sun brings out the birds, and the apple trees, full of flowers, become surrounded by the buzz of lustful bees. Everything seems to breathe fresh and new with life.

A few more minutes to go on the washing machine, and I hope to find the odd pair of socks from the last load so that I might have a matching pair again. Suddenly, a strong ray of sun comes through the open window and I'm looking out at the sky. Did someone play a trick on me or did I really see a sock-shaped cloud up there in the ever-changing sky?

# *My Life in a Box*

Many years ago, I received a very strange blue and green envelope in the mail. My name had been carefully and beautifully handwritten on it. As I opened the envelope, a few bright, colorful paper stars fell from it, and along with them a big key, one of those one would see in some antique museums. There was also a very special scent, similar to my childhood. The envelope did not have a return address, so I was not able to identify the sender. I kept it all in a special place.

Here I am today, not as young anymore, and I feel the compelling urge to tell you the rest of that story. My fingers are moving fast on the keyboard, my head spinning with words and thoughts...

I went to the port yesterday where I usually spend my afternoons. My dog Maya was with me. I sat on my favorite bench, where I read and, from time to time, looked up to watch the ships which came from all around the world. The birds, mostly seagulls, seemed to be welcoming the captains, crews and passengers, flying in circles and making out-of-tune sounds.

Then something unexpected happened. Something unusual was floating, as if dancing, on the waves, slowly making its way closer to shore. After a few moments, it landed very close to where I was sitting. It was one of those trunks people used to send their belongings in while traveling overseas. The trunk was made of faded brown leather with belts around it. And it possessed a lock.

I waited for what seemed hours, though in reality it may have been ten minutes, and watched as no one dared approach the mysterious box. By nature, I am very curious, so I approached the chest with caution. Maya was excited, wagging her tail, jumping all over the place, as if she knew something which I did not.

Suddenly, as I neared the chest, I made out a large label on one of its sides. My name was written there, and in the same handwriting as on that blue and green envelope I had received so many years prior. I guess it's for me, I thought, and began to trouble myself with ways of getting it into my car and back home. Thank God I do not live that far...

The trunk appeared heavy but for some reason, I was able to lift it by myself, and not only that, but I was able to fit it perfectly into the trunk of my car. On my way home, the box began to move, as if something alive were inside. Maya and I were astonished.

A full moon shone, millions of stars sparkling in the sky, anxious to witness what would come next. I ran inside my home and grabbed the envelope with the big key. The key opened the trunk.

Slowly, I lifted the cover. Little stars came flying out from the inside, and that same special scent my old envelope possessed permeated the room. Inside the trunk, I discovered many things, most of them carefully wrapped in newspapers from other countries or delicate tissue paper. Before I began investigating the contents of each bundle, I found a diary. A diary with many pages, all written in calligraphy by the same hand. The first page was a letter intended for me. It read,

My dear great granddaughter,

This is the right time in your life to receive this present from me. I would like you to inherit my belongings, which I have collected over the years. There is a story attached to each one of them. As you will read each story, you will also be able to feel the love, the struggles, the dreams, the hopes, the suffering, the losses, accomplishments, joy and tears, the profound gratefulness for the life I have had on this earth. Open each package carefully. Think about what it meant to me and place it somewhere in your home where Maya will not destroy it. I also was an animal and nature lover as you are. I was also very adventurous and kept a positive attitude most of the time. Sometimes I thought that life was not fair, but my life couldn't have been better. Now it is your turn to prepare a new trunk for your great granddaughter, so she will get to know you even if you are not around.

Include your collection of sheep, your photo albums, your love letters. Write about your family and friends, about those who made you feel special. Write about your struggles, your dreams and hopes, your suffering, your losses and accomplishments, your joys and tears. Send her the key in a special envelope, enclosed with your favorite scent. The envelope will travel to its destination without hesitation. Do not worry. She will get it when the time is right for her. She will also get her trunk, the trunk which you will prepare for her.

All is well. Be in peace. Signed,
Your Great Grandmother

So here I am now, lighting a candle, reading the diary and each one of the stories, enriching my life as I travel my journey on earth.

## *Nenagh (A Place in Ireland)*

How to get inspired?
I heard the question last night
when someone inquired
on a reading rendezvous at a country site.
Writing comes naturally
when you have something or someone in mind
without any special motivation
save what comes from your heart.
Borrow your fingertips to do it
by paper or sophisticated machine
your mind can only expand
in spite of the guilty pile of notes
and things to do, when you think
you do not have the time.
Time to look inside,
time to look outside.
My mind is always moving
with hopes, with dreams, with lights
of many colors, designs, not limited
by the impossible, but triggered
by all there is around.
'The sky's the limit', I take it in often
when in doubt, or
at any time.

## *Astonishment*

*(A Real Story)*

Zoe used to live outdoors. She was happy, she was free, but she was also cold during the winter months. One day, my friend Karli decided it was time to give the cat a new home. Zoe was invited in. Instantly, everybody's life changed. She had two feline brothers and a human mom. She was taken to the veterinarian and got spayed and vaccinated. Zoe was not sure she was liking the new environment and started making herself REALLY at home. In her mind, she was THE QUEEN, and the only one! Her brothers, not used to such a demanding sister, became cautious...and a few weeks later, afraid of her. It was a disaster zone. The brothers had to hide to avoid confrontations, while Zoe was enjoying her new status.

One day, Karli said to me that she could not keep Zoe anymore and gave me the first option to adopt Zoe. My friend did not have to ask twice, and here I was bringing Queen Zoe to my home. Her status was lowered to Lady, and her name became Lady Gata. The first days were very difficult for both of us. She was frustrated because she had to stay indoors. It was raining too much and she did not like swimming. She would jump, out of nowhere, on my back as if I was her prey. OMG, I told myself. Who is this monster?

Slowly, Lady Gata learned some social skills and has become a great companion. I respect her independence and her instincts, and she seemed to be happy until...TODAY!

I was making the beds, which she helps with getting between the blankets, when she suddenly discovered the mirror. WHAT? WHAT? Almost paralyzed looking at her own image, she could not believe there was another cat like her. She stayed there, watching her double, her twin. She did not jump on her own image, and by now, I think she has forgotten such a horrible episode in her life.

Should I change her name to Queen Lady Gata?

# *The Wooden Clog*

I was walking along the river using my walking stick for support. I walked slowly, as spring was coming and I was concentrating on the sounds of the birds. My eyesight is not good anymore but I did see a strange piece of wood passing by. It was tangled in the debris along the bank, as if wanting to escape. I carefully made my way down to the water level to have a closer look and to fish out the piece of wood. It was a wooden clog. When I took it in my hand to have a closer look, it began to talk. I was so surprised that I nearly dropped it back into the water! It said, "The river took me all the way here. I am

I had to sit down, this was all too much for me! But I continued to listen. The clog spoke in almost a whisper: its voice had become hoarse and raspy after being submerged in water for so long. I took a cloth from my bag and dried the wooden clog. I could make out a little laughter as if I were tickling it. Then the clog asked me whether I wanted to hear its story. Curiosity got the better of me, and I said yes. "I have as much time as you need," I told the clog, "I'm not in a hurry. Please, tell me your story."

"Great," the clog replied, and continued:

"I was born of white poplar, a tree which provides the best wood for making shoes. An old shoemaker by the name of Lucas took me into his hands. He had been practicing his craft for a lifetime, a craft so close to extinction it is nearly impossible to find nowadays: cobblery. Lucas was a dedicated and passionate cobbler. He looked at me with a skilled eye and saw my potential. He patted me and chiselled me while listening to classical Music. Mozart was his preferred composer. He had a trademark style which he shared with me, a royal blue and white paint he would apply with fine brushes and a magnifying glass. He decorated me with the most delicate of designs. Whatever he did, he not only used skill but his heart and soul. He carefully carved his signature and the date I was made into the inside of my clog and if you look closely you can make out his name, slightly worn by wear and tear. We were his favorite, my twin and I. Yes, that is how my life as part of a pair of clogs began.

Although difficult to walk in, and so different a style from those heels that are fashionable nowadays, we were very popular with the French (sabots) and the Dutch (klompen). Swedish and Netherland's peasants would use us to protect their feet from dirt and injuries.

Lucas bore a sign over his shop, which repeated his life motto: "Artisans Creating Real Art." One day, he took a load of brand new blue and white clogs, including us, to the local market. A farmer's wife inspected them closely and fell immediately in love with us. She drove a hard bargain with Lucas; it wasn't the first time someone tried to haggle with him. He actually loved the light-hearted banter but knew as well the value of his work, and in the end our creator got his fair price.

The farmer's wife took us home to the farm, where we were put to good use. She was a chubby woman, always with a smile on her face. She spent a lot of time making goodies in the kitchen, and as she had no kids herself, she invited children from her neighborhood to visit and spoiled them with biscuits and cake. You could always identify her, in her red apron with the two big pockets in front, where she kept whatever tools she needed for the job at hand.

Not all of my memories from that time are nice, especially when she wore us to bring the cows in for milking. We walked on rough ground, splashed by cow dung and all kinds of other mysteries I am unable to describe. But I will never forget that awful smell! When the goats' turn for milking came, our lovely blue and white paint was no longer visible. After those crazy beasts were taken care of, the eggs from a few yard-scratching chickens were collected. If you think the smell from cows and goats is bad, well, the stench in the henhouse was almost unbearable, especially on hot days!

The farmer's wife loved gardening and it was the most pleasurable time we had with her, among the seeds and tulips of all colors. She also cared for gardenias, roses, lilies, sunflowers, daffodils, lavender, poppies and daisies. The garden was full of flowers and she just working there. Butterflies, birds, bees and various insects were frequent visitors in her flowering paradise, even the odd red squirrel paid us visits. In the afternoon, she sat under the old oak tree, waiting for her husband's return while sipping a cup of tea and nibbling a few biscuits, enjoying the beauty all around her.

One dark autumn day, a strong storm hit the village with all its might. Grey and heavy clouds, lightning every few seconds, leaves and other light debris blowing in every direction, and then—the sky broke open and the heaviest of rains fell. It was very scary, everything flooded, crops were flattened, and we, along with many others, floated away down the river.

We were not accustomed to such fast and bouncy movements, and I became dizzy and sick. At some point I lost my comrade and somehow continued to float, despite being full of water. I've never seen my 'other' since then, and to tell you the truth no longer know if I'm the right or the left. All that has mattered since then is survival. All I've thought of is reaching a safe and dry harbour.

I travelled day and night. The current took me down long rivers with strange names and through mountainous passes. I floated in salty waters with big waves, cold waters, waters that were wild and these that were calm. I didn't see many others swimming, and whenever I saw a rock and attempted to jump on, a wave or current would whisk me away. I was desperate and very close to giving up, but I was strong, and, as my maker always said, I am made of a very good and sturdy wood.

Once I reached land, a Golden Retriever playing with his owner mistook me for a ball. Holding me in his mouth, he took me to his keeper. I was not looking too well; I was all wet with algae and debris hanging around me. That beautiful dog, which I think was happy to take me to his keeper as a present, was then as puzzled as I with the owner's reaction. The man gave me one short look and, with disgust, threw me back into the water! And there I was again, swimming with the current.

After days floating, I was overcome with a terrible back pain. A hook had gotten stuck in me, and I found myself lifted out of the water and flying towards an old man, standing in the middle of the river with some friends, dressed in what looked like a baggy wetsuit. He also looked at me, expressing some amount of disappointment, and threw me angrily back into the water along with some derogatory words. His drunk buddies laughed until I heard them echoing in my nightmares! I hit a rock and a small crack that looked to be a fracture became part of my body. The water ran through the fissure making my moves even more challenging. Until finally, my lucky day arrived.

You have picked me up, you've let me rest and have dried me with your white handkerchief and now you will surely take me home with you! Now I have a new and different purpose: to be a special ornament, hanging outside of the house, filled with soil as a home for a few tulips you may plant while listening to the music of Mozart!"

And so it was, I brought the clog home and placed it in my garden, where although it no longer was used for walking, it held great purpose. Sometimes I imagined the story she would tell of me someday...

I identified with my new owner in many ways, in part because her life was uprooted as well. She had to leave her home country which she loved so much and still thinks of. She tries so hard to become accustomed to her adopted country. She only speaks broken English, like the one she learned in school which sounded so different from the one spoken in Ireland. 'Hiya'--is it English or Irish? She cannot tell. Not only does she have a language barrier, but she has had to adapt to the weather as well. So much rain, so little sun! All four seasons in one day, sometimes in an hour!

People are so different in Ireland than in her home

country: they drive on the 'wrong' side of the road (or is it actually the right side?), they eat a lot of potatoes cooked so many ways. She sees a tendency in the people of Ireland to protest about nearly everything, and she watches carefully remembering her mother's word: "When in Rome, do as Romans do."

She is determined to be part of the community, she goes to the library, she volunteers with the Youth Association in town, she cares for others and she participates daily! She also has started travelling around the country, giving talks about her experience, about being tolerant and respectful of others, about celebrating our differences, about being human and loving nature. As hard as her first years in Ireland were, she's always grateful to be here, to be alive!

One day, she goes shopping at a local brick-a-brack shop and finds a wooden clog similar to me. The clog is quite deteriorated but she buys it anyway. To her surprise, when she returns home and examines it more closely, she finds that it has the same signature as I do, the signature of Lucas, and the same date as well! The blue and white paint has all but washed off, but there is no doubt, the other shoe is my real companion and we are together again, hopefully forever!

Now a lot of time has passed, and hers is passing, too. She has wrinkles from so much laughter, especially from when she began to understand Irish humor. She has silver threads throughout her hair which she carries proudly. She has some scars, some visible, some not. She has lived!

Romeo, her cat, purrs beside her and her dog Julieta rests by her feet while she reads books in large print. She has some 'spare parts': reading glasses, hearing aids, false teeth. She talks to herself and recently has begun to forget things. Getting is old is not easy. She has a broken hip, the scar looking similar to the fissure I got in my grand adventure. Now she walks slowly, leaning on her walking stick.

She has gone through so much, but she does not complain. She is my angel, she has protected me and I, with every beat of my wooden heart, am telling you how lucky and blessed I am!

# *Lavender and Golf*

It was already quite bright outside so I did not turn on the lights. I threw a woollen jumper on over my white t-shirt and stumbled into the bathroom and—oh my god!—gasped at myself in the mirror. My jumper looked like an 18-hole golf course! Holes of various sizes shone white with the fabric of the t-shirt. I was perplexed, never having experienced a holy jumper before. My in-house advisor in everything Irish informed me that it was the work of moths. Their appetite calls for pure woolen garments. I had never lived on a farm before, let alone owned a collection of woolen cloth.

Subsequently I found out that this busy moth is called Tineola bisselliella, resembles a butterfly, and spends her days silently selecting my prized cloth to chew.

My colander-like sweater had become an inspiration to my curiosity, and I was wondering why sheep do not have holes in their coats, why is processed wool preferred by those little creatures?

Maybe the cat will find some, but in the meantime lavender oil will play a role in the hunt. The heavy smell brings me back to the days when I, totally oblivious to the existence of the Tineola bisselliella, walked the lavender fields in Sequim, Washington.

I will never forget the different tones of purple, and their soft, wave-like movements under the sun. The air was impregnated with their fragrance, another gift from Mother Nature for which to be grateful. Shall I plant some lavender here in Ireland? Will it grow, will it flower and, most importantly, will it fill the wind with its heady perfume?

# *Time is of the Essence*

Lettuce and books,
nature and man-made.
The leaves of one nurture our bodies,
the leaves of the other, our minds.
They both take time, from seed to idea,
to produce and paragraph.
Love also takes time to grow,
from an invisible seed planted
to the fruit of a deep-rooted planet.
While all require patience and perseverance,
love also asks us of the soul and heart.
Our dreams are their nutrients.
Rain, sun and distance,
conditioning endurance,
solid support for our lives.
Love takes us now where we want to be,
love will take us where our dreams lie,
together holding hands we walk the new path ahead
together, our time is perfect,
our time is right.

# *Criollo*

Once upon a time, there were two young natives who loved to explore the jungle, a paradise for adventurous boys like themselves. When light allowed, they would play deep into the jungle with nature and animals that also lived there. Having grown up in the jungle, they were friends of the wild animals, such as the anaconda, jaguar, monkey, colorful macaw, hairy spider and even the crocodile.

One day, they spotted a bird they had never encountered, one of yellow and black feathers. They had never seen a bird of such beauty, and returned to their village to ask the elders about it. The elders informed them that the bird they had seen is called Turpial, the National Bird of Venezuela. When they saw such a bird again, they watched a huge seed fall from its beak, rolling down a hill as if searching for a place to grow. The boys didn't think much of the seed as they were with the bird.

One evening, on their return from a day at the beach, they came upon a group of trees they had never seen before. Curiosity got the better of them and they reached for one of the tree's strange looking fruit which hung from its lower branches. They broke open the shell and were surprised to find big seeds tumbling out from its core. The seeds landed amongst the curious boys, who tossed the fruit aside and continued home.

A few days later, the boys returned to the grove of trees. The seeds which they had abandoned now looked to be an inviting snack. As they were hungry, they split a seed and carefully chewed to determine whether or not it would be edible. To their delight, the seed was delicious. Their mouths, faces and hands were coated in brown, as they had just discovered chocolate!

Needless to say, they spent a lot of time with those trees which they named criollo and became helplessly addicted to. Their tribe became addicted to the sweet taste as well, and eventually that taste became a part of their culture.

The criollo plants continued to grow, spreading far and wide. The custom of sharing a bite of chocolate with family and friends became tradition, and was passed from generation to generation. The story of the criollo made its way across the oceans, as far as Switzerland and Belgium, where a very special and delicate chocolate was produced for the whole world to relish!

All this came to an end when greedy people began cutting down the bushes with their machetes, destroying plantations and everything in their path. They started substituting cocoa beans for coca plants to produce cocaine, a much more profitable crop. Now clouds, dark and threatening, are covering this paradise that once was the playground for those natives and the home of the very best fruit and its famous seeds.

# *The Rock*

Saturday morning, the sun was shining, the waters calm. Everything seemed to be in its place and at peace. I was walking along the beach, contemplating another beautiful day, another gift from nature. The clouds painted the sky in white shapes, changing slowly as if teasing my imagination. I was watching them, remembering how we used to find shapes of animals, smiles, or entire landscapes. I was mesmerized looking up and, not paying much attention, stubbed my toe on a big rock in the sand. OUCH! How did I not see it, it was huge!? For a moment I felt like blaming it for being in my path, but that didn't make much sense.

I sat waiting for the pain to subside, looking out at the ocean. It was right there in front of me, what was I waiting for? I decided the cold water would do some good to my already swollen toe, but I could not bear to go into the icy waves. How can a toe be that important?

I decided to wait a little longer for the pain to dissipate. At least it was not cold or raining. A brown seagull landed close to me, curious to see if I had any bread to share. "No, my friend, I am on a diet," I tell her and offer her a slice of apple. She comes close and takes it from my open hand. I watched while she ate it, enjoying the snack and asking for more. I share a piece which I've already taken a bite of. She doesn't seem to mind, grateful for the food.

The clouds are now rapidly changing, turning greyish. A raindrop falls, and then another, and another. I decided that I must run to the car. Running, I forgot about my toe, now the size of two toes! It had also turned blue. No one was around, except the seagull which flew away in the rain.

# *Shadows*

A silent shadow follows me wherever I go, like a loyal friend who never lets me down. She is with me on my good days and on my bad days. Sometimes she is invisible, hiding behind me. She understands that sometimes I need my space. Sometimes she moves around me. I cannot catch her.

I know she is there, waiting for the right moment to show herself. I feel her, like a reminder that I am not alone in this life. I will always have my own shadow, my own unique extended silhouette. She travels light, does not need an ID or passport. Sometime I feel as if she is the physical image of my vagabond soul, sometimes dancing happily, sometimes crestfallen. Sometimes I like her, sometimes I want her to disappear.

But I cannot rid myself of her. We must go on together until the end.

## *High Expectations*

It was a Tuesday afternoon, May 20th, when young Craig returned home. At that time, he was in fifth grade, and his brother and sister were already in high school. He was a good student and a great little athlete. He was tall for his age and his classmates teased him frequently. In response, Craig fought more often than what his parents would have liked. They were called to the principal's office at least once a month. Craig would be sitting in the office waiting for the reprimand, and also waiting to be taken to the hospital for a broken bone, a bleeding nose, or some other temporary discomfort. Every time, the office visit warranted a signed promise that Craig would not engage in any more fights.

Craig and his parents decided that Craig needed an outlet, and so he started attending martial arts classes with his father. He really enjoyed spending time with his dad, and they became much closer. The Tuesday in question, May 20th, the whole family was set to get together for pizza. A special announcement was to be made. His father, an executive for a large firm, had been offered a job he could not refuse. It included great benefits, a big promotion and, much to the family's surprise, the chance to live overseas.

After consulting with his wife, they decided it would be a worthwhile experience, and little did they know the experience which was in store for them! They had to move that same week, with school beginning the following Monday. This gave them just enough time to say their goodbyes and jump on an airplane which would fly them in Africa.

There was no turning back with the decision. When the older two kids heard the news, they were not very happy. Leaving behind their high school friends was not something they wanted to do. For Craig, it was a different story. His imagination went wild at the thought of Africa, which at the time he believed was a country. Safaris, jungles, animals he had never seen outside of the zoo, strange food and exceptional desserts... He could not contain his excitement with the high expectations he had.

Departure day, the 24th, was an early start for the family. The flight was scheduled for 6:00 a.m. It was Craig's first flight, and a very long one. After a few stops, and twenty-six hours in the air, they finally landed in Africa. What Craig had not realized was that Africa is actually a huge continent and not the country he had imagined!

He was so disappointed. There were no animals, and no jungle. It was hot and humid. They had arrived at Rabat, the capital of Morocco. He could not believe his bad luck. The people didn't even speak English! His expectations vanished and in their place only depression and frustration remained. He immediately wanted to return home.

But he was home, at least for the next two years. And for two years, he did not have to help with cleaning or making his bed. All the chores were done by personnel hired by the company his father worked for.

Time heals even the most profound wounds. A few months into their new life, the family went on a safari that lasted for a few weeks. The trip took them to an animal sanctuary, where chimpanzees, elephants, giraffes, big cats, and all kinds of other animals were loved and taken care of.

On the next vacation, they went to the desert, rode camels and lived with bedouins crossing from town to town, selling all kinds of spices and textiles. The last vacation was exploring beautiful Morocco, a completely distinct culture they had learned to appreciate. After those two years, they had to return to Washington State, and at that point they no longer wanted to go back!

Many years have passed. Craig is now a veterinarian specializing in exotic animals and is planning to go back to the heart of Africa as part of a group called 'Veterinarian Sans Frontiers', who do voluntary work where it is needed most. This time, he is taking his own family along with him. His wife and two teenage daughters appear hesitant about the move. But in the end, their adventure does not disappoint.

# *Contrast*

Not that long ago, in a country where I once lived, there was a Department for Peacemaking. The Minister was in charge of Conflict Resolution, which was never abandoned until peace existed on both sides of the conflict. They also had the mission to nurture the seed of humanity, to raise awareness around the earth and awaken consciousness to a better world.

There was a country on the other side of the ocean, which had, in stark contrast, a Minister for Justice-War-Making. His office was in charge of promoting wars whenever and wherever possible. Crises evolving from legal or ethical issues were skillfully used to enable weapon manufacturers to make a financial killing. It must be said that this Minister was very successful in his position; the citizens of his country constantly lived in fear of another armed conflict. It was almost like he had an addiction to blood.

These two countries, whose two very powerful forces could not have been more opposite, each had citizens who reflected the actions of their leaders. Citizens of some smaller countries trying to survive the actions of war started to migrate toward more peaceful territories. Some families did so by foot, as the pilgrims of all times have, some by train where they were pushed off and trapped, some by refrigerated trucks used for the transport of meat, others by boat. Survival wasn't their only motivation, they wanted to thrive!

One day, my mother took me to a boat. It was one of those rubber yellow ones and it looked quite sturdy. I was little and oblivious to what was going on around me. This trip seemed to be an adventure. The sun was burning down on us, the choppy waves making the boat jump up and down so it felt like a rollercoaster ride. The splashes of salty water refreshed my face and slowly I became soaking wet. I was having so much fun, all the while my mother sat silently. She seemed to be fighting back her tears in an attempt to hide them from me. I did not know why, but when I saw her joining her hands in prayer, the seriousness of our journey became clear to me.

The day passed and night fell slowly. We still had some canned food to eat and fresh water to drink. The sea was calm that night, and the soft movement of the boat reminded me of the hammock we had at home. I loved it so much that I often fell asleep in it. Besides myself, there were a few other children travelling along, but we were kept from speaking with one another. Silence between us hung like a dark shadow.

The next day at sea, some people started to get sick and the captain got rid of them, one by one. I was horrified. People were screaming as the boat moved away. Fewer people to care about, more space for us, said our 'captain' ironically. This happened day after day, and sometimes at night.

On the fifth day my mom got sick and our turn came. We were both thrown overboard. We spent many hours floating, exhausted from holding our heads above the waves, and were at the point of giving up when a vessel came to our rescue. Once aboard, I fainted.

When I awoke, I did not know how much time had passed. My mom was by my side, and we were not at sea anymore. I did not understand who the people were around us; we were in a foreign country whose people spoke a language I did not understand. We were safe, no longer hungry or thirsty, and so grateful.

We were not the only ones at the camp, many families were sheltered there as well. The community of refugees was prepared to adapt, we were ready to assimilate into our new home, to start a new life in the country that was home to the Minister for Peace-Making.

Slowly, we newcomers felt at home. This new humane attitude benefited us all, and good deeds came back around. The message was spread, the gratefulness of the forced migrants (or refugees, as others define us) turned into a swell of motivation, skills and achievements. These came from respect, tolerance, positive affirmation, and ethics, which became models for the world to follow. And the world began to change!

# *The Cat at the Plaza*

An old windmill on the little hill catches my attention, its arms spinning slowly, as if burdened by their age, its inner workings sighing. Still the mill functions after more than one hundred years of turning nonstop, provided there is enough wind. In front of the windmill stands an iron bell, another antique. Both grew old together, years having taken their toll as the elements weathered the stories written onto their bodies.

The bell brings memories to my mind, for all my life I have heard bells ringing: calling me to classes, cathedrals reminding the peasants and passers-by the time of the day, on Sundays the powerful calling of the worshippers to mass.

This fishing town has a lovely square and across from the mighty church there is a small coffee shop where I take a break. A huge cat slowly walks towards me. It looks like a streetwise tomcat, and the cat-lover in me is pleased. Now he changes direction and takes residence on the stairs leading to the little coffee shop, apparently happy with himself and the world around him. His eyes are not fully closed; he observes everything around him, waiting for a few scraps to fall off of one of the tables.

I went to the counter for another espresso, leaving my notebook on the table behind me, and when I returned I found it scarred with cat's claws. I knew that these scratches were telling the story of the tomcat's life, so I grabbed my feline-to-human dictionary and transcribed it thus:

Meow, meow, here is my story:

I was born in Portugal, I believe, about eleven years ago but really who can be sure of that. It feels as if I've been here forever. I've never met my father but I remember having three siblings. When the time came, we took very different roads. My only brother always felt he was special, because he was born half an hour earlier. His long, ginger-colored hair was real cute. He was adopted fast and now lives in a mansion. He doesn't leave the premises except to be groomed and to visit the vet, which he hates because he was neutered there. Sometimes I wonder whether he knows what he is missing. If you think I'm fat you should see that guy, he can hardly walk!

My two calico sisters also found a new home; they now live in an old monastery with even older nuns. Last time I saw them they looked a bit on the thin side, so my guess is there aren't very many mice around there.

And me? I am the free-spirited one, wandering around the town nearly all the time. I have a few scars, and not everyone likes what they call a 'stray' cat. I was limping for a while after being hit by a car. I am missing a good bit of my right ear, it really did hurt when Felix, the black cat of the neighborhood got his teeth into it! But all that doesn't stop me, life at the square is unthinkable without me. I'm walking slow, rubbing my tail on tourists' legs, making friends and avoiding enemies. As I get older, fighting with the other cats isn't as fun as it used to be.

I'm still a fabulous athlete. To reach my bed, I have to cross a major road and that's no easy task. I really have to speed up to make it safely to the other side. One of my many friends was not fast enough one night and ended up a stamp in the road. Life can end at any moment! I'm also still good at jumping and climbing, so I can walk the roofs at night and spend long hours chasing birds. They are hard to catch but sure are tasty.

# *Another Extraordinary Day*

If I just keep my eyes open, I can turn boredom into excitement. I have no time to waste. The sound of an aquaplane catches my attention and I lift my view from the notebook where I am writing these notes.

An old man is walking alone with his walking stick, looking down. He notices that I am watching him, then makes eye contact and smiles. I smile back, inviting him to sit by my side.

We start talking. I notice a little bit of an accent (as if I didn't have one!), and I recall one of my professors suggesting to hold onto it. "It is part of your identity," he said, "and it will open many doors." He was right. My accent has helped break the ice on occasions where it felt as if I was inside a glacier.

So, going back to my story with my gentle old man, I notice numbers tattooed on his arm. They are the identification numbers of people at the concentration camps, and he is one of them.

His younger days were a real struggle and he lost everything, literally everything: his family and friends, his toys and books...he was stripped naked. Only his voice was familiar to him, so he would talk words of encouragement, his own words, his own survival kit.

A cargo ship is passing by. We look at it. Tears start falling from his eyes, tears of pain, but also tears of gratitude.

He talks about the day he finally heard other voices, the voices of freedom, directing him to a ship similar to the one we are watching. The ship is leaving soon, going far away. He looks at a mirror and can not recognize his own self; only bones and wrinkled skin cover his body.

Accepting help from strangers is not something he is used to. Humbled, he starts smiling again. He learns a new language, our common language of survival.

And here we are today, talking as if we were old friends, as if we knew each other from before. We share losses, and we share hope. We are not strangers anymore.

# *The Free-Spirited Bee*

Did I wake up early today? I'm not quite sure. I can only remember that it was just beginning to get light outside. The fog was lifting from the valley, and the trees were starting to take their form. All was covered in an energetic calm.

My steps to the barn gently broke the morning silence. From the barn, a different noise, rare but not unknown to these still mornings. A newborn calf, looking at me with its deep black eyes and soft curls, wobbling in the indecision of taking her first steps. She was not quite safe on her legs but she was eager to be nurtured by the warmth and sweet milk of her mother. I smiled, tempted to go in and wrap my arms around her, but held back, warned by the mother's stern way of protecting this new life.

Now birds are coming in from their resting places, some early flowers have begun decorating the yard with their color, inviting bees to a cup of pollen. In my mind, I play the game of pretending that I am a bee, flying free and working hard. My free-spirited self tempts me again, and here I am making a detour before returning to my hive. Explore further next time, an inner voice urges.

Curiosity gets ahold of me and I buzz to the barn where Nena, the new calf, stands uneasily. "Welcome to this world," I whisper in her ear, landing softly on her downy flanks. Whap! Her tail swats my fragile bee body, sending me against the slatted wall. Dizzy, I fall down, where a giant, mud-caked hoof stamps me into a smear, ending my short but joyous life.

And then I wake up!

# *Deja Vu*

My daughter just sent me this quote: "I only have one life to live, but in books I can live a thousand lives," —Rasht, Iran. Great truths reside in it!

I was walking in the streets of the small town where I live and I decided to enter a second-hand bookstore, having nothing special in mind. It was one of those moments when you are where you are, just to be! So, I started to look at the book covers, one by one, reading on the back cover of each story.

One in particular caught my attention. It was the story of a girl who had a difficult life in everybody else's eyes but her own. The book was written in the eighteenth century and took place in Europe. It seems to be one of those books that inspires you, a real story. The cover was nothing special, it was green and purple with some yellow, all combined, showing a rather pale silhouette of a girl smiling, running in the rain with her grey Weimaraner dog towards a castle with a magnificent big tree in the background. The very vivid image was captured so well by the illustrator, I bought the book.

At home in our living room, accompanied by Ghost, my grey Weimaraner dog, I was curled up in my rocking chair, the crackling open fire creating the right atmosphere to get lost in my new book. While skimming the pages I sensed the musty smell you only get from old books, and suddenly a yellow leaf fell out of the book; a leaf from a Ginko tree that looks like a very small fan, like a beautiful fine triangle, exactly like the leaf I had picked up and placed inside the book I was reading at that time.

I was with Kim, at a park in Germany. She had pointed out a big Ginko tree, the oldest tree in that public garden. We could see the ruins of a castle close to the lake, benches to rest on and to admire the squirrels jumping from branch to branch. I picked up a pamphlet, one of those written for tourists which narrated the story of the family who lived in the castle. I kept the flyer in my backpack and stored it in the closet while waiting for the next opportunity to travel.

All this came vividly back to me when the leaf fell out of my "new" very old book. Something was becoming too familiar in my mind. I then dug into my backpack and to my surprise, the picture of the ruined castle was an exact copy of the castle on the cover of the book, and there was the magnificent big Ginko tree, in the same place I remembered. The leaf I had kept from my walk and the leaf inside the book were twins, and now I was able to live the story as if I were witnessing it.

"Ghost," I said, "is this coincidence or was it meant to mean something?"

He looked at me with his big eyes, and did not respond. There was no answer.

## *Green*

A high school classmate of mine always wore a green shirt. It was like a symbol, worn as a uniform, as a sign for something. He was very introverted and altogether quite intelligent. I always had a crush on him, though I kept it a secret. It was one of those unrequited loves you hold near to yourself and never let go of. Nobody dared ask him about his green shirt. I am sure that he had more than one, but during our graduation ceremony he wore his most-loved green shirt, which he took off and threw into the air in place of a graduation cap. As the sky rained black caps and tassels, I grabbed the soft green shirt and kept it for myself.

Many years went by, and I never threw that shirt away. For some reason, I knew it was worth keeping around. One day, I landed a job in a neighboring town. As I was packing, I found the green shirt washed and folded in a plastic bag, tucked into an old trunk I'd inherited from my grandmother. Along with the trunk, I'd inherited many of my grandmother's belongings within it. Forgotten and never-used, I did not want my keepsakes to end up like hers.

Several years later, I called my friend of the green shirt. He had graduated from college and was in town for the weekend. We decided to meet at a new coffee shop in town, unique for its appeal to the locals. It had the perfect atmosphere for more than a handshake.

The icebreaker was his t-shirt, which I had brought to our encounter. I wanted to know the story behind it, and when I took it from its plastic wrapping and laid it on the table, he told me.

It was a shirt which had belonged to his father, whom he had loved dearly. When his father went to war, he left behind a small package for his son to open if he did not return. Years passed, and it became clear that the package was to be opened. A note on the inside said, 'My son, this green t-shirt might not be much, but it means a lot. It is made of a rare material which will protect you from the rain and the wind, it will protect you from the sun as well. You will feel my arms around you when needed, and my hands pushing you when you are challenged to take the next step. Pass it on after your graduation. I promise you, it will return to you with greater gifts.'

Now the future is the present, and we stand, face to face, with the green shirt between us. I could not hold back my affection any more, why would I? I'd had the green shirt, now I have the green light!

## *Noises*

I hear some faint but strange noise in the old house.
I don't believe in ghosts. Are those heavy raindrops
falling on the skylight? Maybe one of the many
magpies is dancing around on the roof? Then clack!
Another trap has been triggered and a small life is gone.
But I have never jumped on a chair so fast! Fearing another
to be lurking around, a broom comes in handy,
as if actually a magical weapon, ready to defend me
from the fast-moving four-legged creature more than a
hundred times smaller than myself.
Where does my fear come from? Our so-called
'modern life',
that disconnection from nature? I have little in common
with these furry critters which, against all odds, share their
lives in this old house, trying to survive.
I can think of others from the animal kingdom
that I'd prefer to share a home with.
And there—I can hardly believe my eyes!—I see it:
another ratoncito comes by, strutting slowly,
oblivious of me still standing on the chair.
There and then I decide, in spite of all my
well-intentioned musings, that I will change
the broom for a cat!

## *Gummy Bears*

Some time ago, a little boy named Oliver decided it was time to make one of his secret dreams come true. The day before, he had gone with his mom and baby brother to the birthday party of one of his classmates. The children played all afternoon, and at the end he had returned home with a bag of gummy bears. He loved them and wanted to eat them all, but remembered that it was late and that he wasn't allowed to eat sugar before bedtime.

While dreaming that night, he had a vision. The vision entangled the sweet gummy bears with a story of magical beans he had heard in class earlier that day. When he awoke, he knew that it was time to make his dream come true, and he knew just how to do it.

"Mom, mom!" he cried, pulling on her skirt. "I need your help. Tell me, can I use that abandoned pot lying in the yard?"

"Of course you can, Oliver," she replied, then watched from the window as he cleaned the pot and filled it with compost. To her surprise, he then planted the gummy bears in the moist soil. In his mind, they would grow into a gummy bear plant, high and strong for he and his friends to climb during his own birthday celebration.

Oliver's mom went to him and said, "Oliver, sometimes dreams come true, but you need to be patient. You need to believe in them. You need to visualize them, to nurture and share them. They are like any other gift you receive or give, but for now it is a gift of your imagination."

Seasons passed, and a few birthday celebrations as well, but Oliver did not forget his dream. One summer, Oliver's family decided to build a porch in front of their house, and Oliver had to move his gummy bear pot to the greenbelt in the backyard.

One winter morning, when all was covered in snow, a colorful branch emerged from the ground. It came from Oliver's pot! It grew, and grew, and grew. There was music from the forest celebrating the event. It was a different tree, a tree with gummy bears on its branches.

The news ran throughout the town. Newspapers covered the phenomenon. Children came to play and eat endless colorful bears off the tree. Oliver became an inspiration for those who had lost faith in their dreams. He had never lost his!

# *Sea Sons*

The seasons come in waves, sometimes abruptly, sometimes in soft movements. For the sons of the sea, the seasons grow, invade, challenge. The sons may adapt, they may die or renew, they learn to survive, and they come back as if returning to work left unfinished.

Mother Nature will ask. She will demand. The disobedient Niño competes with the unruly Niña, both careless and immature, disrespectful of the boundaries between life and death, causing destruction as they pass through.

Mother Nature called both to a meeting. The meeting was set for the 21st of June, summer solstice. ('Solstice' comes from the Latin words 'sol', meaning sun, and 'sistere', meaning to come to a standstill). Mother Nature hopes the kids will stand still and listen well.

"My children," said Mother Nature, "it is time to make some important decisions. You have been playing out-of-control for too many years and in that you have caused devastation and hunger around the world. Many animal species have become extinct, others have lost their homes, even others have lost their hopes." Nina, quick with words, responds,

"We are just playing the game with the humans, a game we do not like playing but we have no choice. They are sending us smoke signals from their industries. They have changed the course of rivers and we have lost the guidance of our maps. They have cracked the soils with giant machines until the earth bleeds. The blood is thick and black, and we cannot move in it." The Niño continues sadly,

"We feel they are cheating and we want to save the Earth. We are shaking up the game to see if we can find our pieces again. My sister and I feel devastated, but the humans give us no other choice."

The wise Mother sat in silence for a moment. The words of the children resonated with her; she understood them. It is like a vicious cycle, one being the consequence of the other. Niño, Niña and Humans are intertwined so strongly that they are not able to act any differently.

A Universal Consensus was then agreed upon between the Sun, the Moon, the Waters and Winds, the Rivers and Mountains, the Volcanoes and the Oceans, Forests and Plains, and also between all the diplomats of the world. They all needed a break, they conceded, and so they came to a common understanding and committed plan. Mother Nature concluded the meeting with these words:

"I have survived fire and ice, and I will survive again. It is in your hands. Be responsive, be responsible. Your own children will have a better life, a better present, and the best future." And with these words, she rested her case.

# *The Bridge*

Out of the blue, right in front of me, a beautiful and tempting suspension bridge...

It is very wide and I am admiring how safe it looks and feels.

I can see green tree tops below, the eagles flying around as if inviting me to cross. A warm wind is blowing. It is a pleasant and clear day and everything seems to be in place; just the slightest trace of an unsettled emotion lingers within me. I cannot describe it. Something is pushing me to start crossing this bridge. My hands hold on to the rail. Why am I always so adventurous, why do I want to keep moving, why do I need to take risks..., haven't I taken enough of those in my life? Why didn't I just stay at home today, contemplating the day going by, serene, soft, surrounded with familiar sounds and smells, with the comfort of the touch of my partner's hands.

My inner voice chimes in again, and much like the story of the enchanting sirens, it is urging me to move on.

I trust my gut feeling... and... again... I ask myself, why not?

From far away beckons the unknown.

I start walking, slowly, one step at a time, enjoying this perfect day (or, so I assume).

Suddenly, I notice that the bridge is narrowing a little and I am guessing it has something to do with engineering, something about weight and distance. I do not know. It feels normal to me. I continue.

A cold wind starts blowing, and, I find myself trapped in the middle of the overpass. I have walked only half of the bridge. I am scared. The bridge that seemed so safe is now swaying, up and down, side to side, rather violently. I am holding on tight. I am forced to get on my hands and knees and crawl like a baby learning how to walk. I look behind me to the end of the bridge from where I started. The structure has disappeared. I feel like I am in the midst of an awful dream, a nightmare, alone. Just stopping and staying still is far too risky. I cry for help, but nobody answers my call. The rain starts falling. Now I am crying. My tears mix with the raindrops and I realize that I am soaking wet. My hands slip. The rail has vanished. Only a zip line remains.

In that very moment I realize that I either have to reach safety or I will die—reality; it is as simple as that.

I hear myself reminding myself: "I do not want my life to be over, I love my life!"

I take a deep breath.

At this point I am hanging from a fine line. My arms are strong. I can do it. I have to do it. I have no other choice.

First I move one hand, hold on tight—just keep moving. Then I move the other hand—one hand at a time. Slow progress...

It feels like an eternity. It is not fun at all.

Behind me, nobody is waiting for me any more—and ahead of me, who knows?

I have now finally reached the other side of the bridge. I have actually made it. I had to do it.

I still do not know why.

# *Grandfather and Grandson*

Grandpapito and Grandmamita are getting older and are starting to have some health issues that they did not have before. They are starting to have difficulties walking, hearing, eating without teeth, seeing without glasses, holding things with their hands. Their body parts, as in any part of a machine, are starting to malfunction. New parts are too expensive for their budget or cannot be replaced.

They are wise. They have been sharing their stories at home, a different story for each person. It has been like customized storytelling for people, because they know not everyone will appreciate the same ones. Grandpa will share stories of hunting, of fishing and protecting, of healing. Grandma will share stories of cooking, weaving, basket-making, and of family. They know they are almost ready to transition into a spiritual world where they will experience new sensations, but while they know that now, they know too that they must stay on earth for the time being.

One day, a grandson comes to visit. He is listening to a story, but is too young to understand. The old man asked him, "What are you up to today?"

"Nothing," says the boy. Not very happy with such a response, grandfather asked another question,

"What are you doing tomorrow?"

"Nothing." The wise old man then replies, "Tomorrow, when the sun starts showing behind that mountain, be ready. You are coming with me."

The next morning, as soon as the sun rose, grandpa was at the grandson's house. "Let's go, let's go!" says the boy, excited to be the only one going along.

They walked, and as they spotted many animals along the path, the elder told stories of eagles and squirrels, rabbits and coyotes. They also talked about the responsibility to care for grandma, because he, grandpa, would be leaving soon.

A few hours passed, and grandpa and grandson arrived at the shore of the Klallam River. Papa threw a line in, and not too long after, caught a fish. He showed his grandson how it was done: two, three, four more fish. The boy wanted to fish all evening, but wise grandpa said in a clear voice, "Listen, my boy, and listen carefully: do not take more than what is needed. You might need more tomorrow."

They returned home in silence, the five fish for their family slapping against their legs.

Some years went by, and grandpa left for the next journey. The boy was left to care for his old grandma, who told him that she would also be gone soon. They would soon be looking after the grandson, sparking his memory, passing their stories onto his children, keeping their traditions alive and honoring those who came before us all.

# *Moss and the Magnifying Glass*

*"If you do not know where you are going, any road will take you there."* –Lewis Carroll

Snuggling up beside the campfire with my beloved mutt, I gazed into the flames whose hypnotic and calming effects were inescapable. I thoroughly enjoyed the comfort of my brand new, royal blue sleeping bag, big enough to turn inside without getting tangled up. It is a new generation of bags, created for people who love their comfort and enjoy adventure at the same time. And the dog on my lap enjoyed it, too. In no time at all, we were both asleep.

When I awoke hours later, my dream remained so vivid in my mind that I decided to write it down before it escaped and faded into oblivion…

I didn't know where I was or where I was going. I was walking briskly with my two sticks (reminiscent of my recent Camino walk) and suddenly I found myself sitting on a fallen tree trunk. Someone must've cut off some wood because I clearly saw the annual rings, telling me their story.

I could see the good years through their fat, big rings, and I saw the frugal years which left barely a trace, a thin remembrance. I tried to count them (no easy task) but I stopped when I saw that this tree was clearly much older than me.

Suddenly I was holding a magnifying glass in my hand and examining a little crack which was not discernible to the naked eye. The crack opened wider and wider, and I looked deep, my curiosity getting the better of me. Suddenly, I found myself in the middle of a green oasis, a beautiful miniature replica of the world but without a trace of the effects of humans. There was an overwhelming feeling of harmony, peace and tranquility.

Moss covered most of this world, hills and prairies carpeted the land in strange patterns, some like golf courses, others resembling organic farms. A good few were covered in daisies, lavender and tulips, others with fruit trees and vegetables. Insects and animals roamed this paradise, coexisting in harmony.

I was fascinated by the ancient mosses which survived the Ice Ages, thousands of seasons, and are home to so many creatures. Growing on rocks and trees they will continue to survive. Rain had formed small lagoons where lady birds played and larger animals drank. There were no roads as far as the eye could see, but there were many well-worn footpaths. Whoever lived there must walk constantly, I thought. There were no sounds from cars or motorcycles, factories or of weapons. The only noise came from the little birds' harmonious melodies, and from the water rushing in streams and jumping over moss-laden rocks.

Suddenly my Fairy Godmother appeared out of nowhere, took my hand and guided me as we flew over this magical land, one that, she explained, had been secretly guarded from the humans. "This is the way your world would look if people did not fight against nature," she said. "Remember, nature can live without men, but men cannot live without nature. Nature will survive. It is generous. Everything you need is here for you. Spread this message when you return to your home." With that, she accompanied me to the tree where I entered, and placed a drop of honey-like liquid beneath my tongue.

When I woke up I noticed that the fire I had slept by had burned down. A yellowish piece of paper was hanging from my pack, the words written in the ash left from the fire. It was a note signed by my Fairy Godmother, with the same message she relayed before, a reminder for me to keep. Holding the paper in my hand, I was not sure if I were still dreaming or if I had indeed awakened.

# *When*

When you walk in the park and see children
jumping around,
laughing, you ask yourself, where did my childhood go?
When you see the young playing at the beach,
singing and playing guitars around the fire pit,
you ask yourself,
where did my adolescence and young adult years go?
When you visit a college campus, taking your own
children who consider
studying there, you ask yourself, where did those years go?
When you see couples holding hands, looking into
each other's eyes,
communicating with their hearts, you ask yourself,
where did our magic go?
When I awoke this morning, these question's answers
came to me:
All those years are in my heart, in my memories,
they are in my soul.
Now I realize, more than ever, that every minute counts,
and I will never let any of them go!

## *Mom*

A soft rain is falling and the sun has nearly disappeared behind the mountains. Night is coming fast. This morning I woke up very early and am now tired. A good sleep will charge my batteries with energy for tomorrow. The rain is falling even heavier now and I begin to pick up my pace; crossing a road where kids usually wait for their bus beneath a small shelter. It is dark there now and the bench is dry. The last thing I remember is the monotonous drumming of raindrops on the metal roof. In no time I begin to sleep.

Suddenly, a rainbow arcs out of the foothills. Little angels are playing on it, sliding down its long sides, landing on the grass and flying again to the top. Their laughter is contagious and is heard around the earth, carefree and happy.

The rain is no longer made of precipitation but instead of tiny, hand-written messages from the angels. One lands beside me and I open it. It has my mother's handwriting and it reads, "My daughter, I will always love you with all of my heart. Mothers never abandon their children. Even from where I am now, I watch over you. I am one of the stars you can see on a clear night." I now remember her wise pieces of advice, which always proved to be true.

Upon awakening, the rain has stopped. The moon, just rising now, meets the sky full of sparkling stars. One in particular is much brighter than the others and I wonder... is it my mother's presence?

In deep thought I make my way toward home, knowing my mom has always been beside me. Whenever I have had make a decision, I have always asked myself, what would mom think about this? And I can hear her saying, Why not? Go where your heart takes you, let your dreams guide you and you will always be right. If you don't try you will never know if it was the right thing to do.

By the time I reached home the full moon has almost completed its journey. I changed into my pajamas, waving at the stars and saying a little prayer for all the mothers watching over their loved ones tonight.

# *Wheels*

Photographer Diane Arbus once said, "My favorite thing is to go where I've never been," and, to a certain extent, I can relate. I love to go to new places, try new foods, meet new people and, most of all, learn of different cultures. But I also enjoy returning to my own path and living it day-to-day. The memories from the past, though not all joyful, inform my present experience with colorful images.

Recently, I found a Facebook post which stated, "I'd rather have a passport full of stamps than a house full of stuff." I would love to add: 'I'd rather have a diary full of memories than a blank page waiting to be filled.' My hand writes everyday, the ink flowing across the paper as the brush of the artist does to his canvas.

Having said that, there was a time, a very long time ago, when I learned to ride a bicycle. The bike had two big wheels and two small ones in the back for balancing and stabilizing the larger ones. A few weeks ago, when visiting my dad, he was also on four wheels, two big ones and two smaller ones, but instead of a bicycle, these wheels belonged to a wheelchair. There he sat, gazing at the horizon, he eyes lost in time and space but still possessing those shining sparkles of recognition for a familiar word, gesture, hug or laughter.

While the bicycle gives you freedom, the wheelchair restrains. Like wheels, my spirit turns and turns, until the breaks of age will slow its cycle. Like wheels, our bodies need maintenance. Our 'parts' are made to last a lifetime, but use (if not abuse!) and age take their toll. Like wheels, we also find ourselves caught in potholes from time to time, trapped in sand and mud, sliding across the slippery roads and challenged to move forward. Like wheels, we travel and rotate around our own world, making our own histories. But unlike wheels, we have the option to break out and go our very own way.

## *The Missing Piece*

In a distant green country with magical mountains and rivers which sing as if they were caressing the rocks with their voices, the birds enrichen the sky, the trees whisper as if sharing secrets, rabbits hustle, and flowers thicken the air with their delicate and complex scents. This is where Opa lives, a lonely farmer, a man so special he is difficult to describe in words. His heart is bigger than his chest, his able hands transform wood into magnificent pieces of art. He is generous to a fault, but he is not happy. It seems as if he were walking around his head, spreading down his body in a web-shaped shadow which only allows timid rays of sunshine to filter through in tangled threads.

One day, one of Opa's granddaughters, a cute little girl with curly blonde hair, very fond of puzzles, brings one to her grandfather. It is a puzzle made especially for him. They place it on top of a wooden table and begin to put it together. Several weeks pass, and it is almost finished when they realize that one of the very important pieces is missing.

Opa also realizes that the puzzle is the image of his own farm, containing everything: the tractors, flowers and cats, even his own image shrouded in the cloud. They search among every piece in the box, under all the furniture, in every place they can think of, but cannot find the missing piece. They desperately try other pieces from other puzzles, but none fit.

Meanwhile, in a nearby village, a retired teacher has opened a puzzle shop. The teacher is an intelligent and loving woman, who enjoys many things: children, animals, nature, singing, writing and cooking. She always keeps biscuits in her puzzle shop. The children of the town love to go there, where puzzles await them on a long wooden table. Every now and again a stray piece falls to the floor, and so the teacher creates a box in which to put wayward pieces.

Opa and his granddaughter decide to go to her puzzle shop, where they ask the teacher about the missing piece. She directs them toward her box of spare and missing pieces, and as soon as the farmer and the girl approach it, they see the missing piece. It nearly jumps out at them as they pick it up, startled, and take it to its rightful place.

The piece possesses the image of a woman, familiar looking, and Opa places it gently into the puzzle, where it fits perfectly. He and his granddaughter laugh in their accomplishment and relief. Suddenly, the puzzle begins to shine, to shake like the trees shake in the wind and to whisper like the rivers whisper in their rocky beds. The woman's face breaks into a smile and they recognize then the same expression of the woman at the puzzle shop. It is she!

Without thinking, and with the piece now in his hand, the farmer and granddaughter return to the puzzle shop and find her, smiling behind her counter with a biscuit in her hand. Opa reaches out his hand, as if breaking through the fog that has enveloped him for so long. As they make their way toward the farm, the dark clouds light up as if by magic.

# *Dragons in Love*

A dragon was born in New York City and Sparky was
his name.
He had blue eyes, a huge heart and wings to help him fly
to reach his dreams and turn them into real life.
Summers and winters passed, as did autumns and springs
and just by will of God (or perhaps Chance?)
Dragonella showed up.
Their eyes met only once and then many more times
their fire kept them warm, their souls combined.
A grey cloud with high winds, a stormy tornado, arrived
throwing them all over the earth, confusing their ways,
separating their faith. He stayed north,
she went south. A long time passed since that
disastrous event.
The sun might be coming again, dusting the eyelashes
of Dragonella's
big brown eyes and stoking the fire still burning
in her heart.
One day, she dreamed that her dragon Sparky
had come back
and serenaded her playing his beautiful guitar,
singing 'Puff the Magic Dragon'
and 'The first Time Ever I Saw Your Eyes',
songs they both enjoyed, which sealed their path
of flying together and sharing their dreams alike.

# *Frogs and Drums*

After showing my friend Patrick this beauty area of the Pacific Nowthwest where I am blessed to live, we came back home. We spent the day hiking with my dog Rita, - who never seemed to get tired. She has the energy of many of us together. We also watched sailing boats, canoes and kayaks playing in the water, eagles, blue herons and many more birds flying in the skies. Wild flowers of many colors blooming that seemed to be dancing with the soft wind that was caressing them. When we opened the door, an unexpected card fell on the floor. It said: "You will be coming tonight". We both read it. The words on the card disappeared and just a paper made of flowers and seeds remained. We did not know what to think. Had a glass of red wine, crackers and cheese, and went to sleep. It was after midnight, and the sound of a wind chime awakened us. Frogs and distant drums were in tune, making this rhythmic music as if talking to each other. Boom boom...quic quic...boom quic... Time to go..., but where? We started walking under the full moon. The starts were blinking like Christmas lights. We arrived at the shore of a body of water. A lightweight narrow canoe was waiting for us. We jumped in it, as did Rita, my inseparable and loyal companion. Every time the paddles kissed the water bioluminescence, gave us the sensation of glowing water emerging as the underwater currents guided us to our destination. The water was calm.

It looked like a lake, but it was the sea. We arrived at an island where the Chemakums were gathered around a fire. We were the only guests, and we had to stay as quiet as we could. The drums continued loud and coordinated for some time, and then…silence. An older man and an older woman began speaking. They talked about their history, their traditions, their pride, their ancestors. They talked in such incredible voices, sharing their lives with us. Some were loud, some like whispers. Their stories were so vivid that you could almost see them happening in front of your eyes. Magic. The fire started dying, the drums saying their farewells, and we knew it was time to go back. Jumped again on the canoe. The moon had gone to sleep. The sun was announcing the dawn. At home, again, I made coffee and foamed milk. Sip…sip… I tried to start typing about our experience and what we learned, but the computer did not help. I then tried to hand write the information, but the ink disappeared. Of course, now I remembered what the old couple said: "Oral traditions should be kept intact. You should talk to your children, tell them your stories, tell them about your family, tell them about the magic of life. Put your electronics away when you get home and embrace family life again. Become story tellers of your own history. The time with your people should be magic time. Do not waste it". I have a few stories to tell…

## *The Venezuelan Porcupine*

I am in bed, trying to sleep a few hours. A loud noise I can hardly understand wakes me. Halting words almost illegible, coming from someone wearing a red beret, are spreading the news that water service will be provided for only one hour to our community.

I rush to the bathroom before the minutes vanish. I haven't taken a shower in more than a week and I only have 55 minutes (it feels like 55 seconds!). I also have to start the washing machine. I do not use my china anymore and do not like to accumulate dirty dishes on the sink. I had to change my habits and now I use paper plates. The handles in the shower have not been used in a while and they are getting rusty. I breath and try to turn them on again. They finally surrender and I am hoping to feel the cold water emerge from the holes of the showerhead. Cold, of course. (We have not had power in more than a month and candles have become one of our best friends. Drops start to fall slowly on my head. Finally, a spritz of water lasting less than 5 minutes and then... That was all for the day, or for the week. My clothes did not get washed, are covered with a bit of soap I bought at the black market. I go back to bed, frustrated, angry, feeling powerless and sad.

I fall asleep again, I am exhausted. In my dreams I remember the days where I lived in a free country, where I had the choice of taking showers in the morning or at any time of the day. I had soap and shampoo. I even had toothpaste. I have almost forgotten the fresh and agreeable taste of it.

My dream suddenly turned into a nightmare. I was again under the shower, waiting for the water to bath my face and my body. Instead, iron nails came shooting at me. Blood came falling from my head. The pain was unbearable. An immense sorrow and sadness mixed with my tears running down my cheeks. I could not stop them. I dropped on my knees and started to pray. I now looked like a porcupine, or maybe like a gigantic spiked collar. Was this a sign I needed to protect myself now? How could I have been so naïve?

My alarm clock is ringing. I touch my body, and it is soft as always. My hair is clean. I ran to the bathroom. I turned the lights on and I used my toothbrush with mint toothpaste. I washed my hands and face with warm water. My clothes, cleaned and ironed are hanging in my closet.

# *Why?*

Why now? Why not closer?
Why, why, why?
There are so many why's
and so few answers. Will they change
our destiny? Will they change what is right?
I am embracing my blessings,
they are so many, I have lost count.
A new life is waiting, welcoming us with open arms,
to walk together in our autumns, our winters,
springs and summers.
Looking into each other's eyes,
holding hands, laughing and crying,
dancing and singing with the stars,
smelling the earth bathed in rain,
enjoying the sun with each day,
listening to the symphony of nature,
tasting the fruits with delight.
Humbled, I honor you, my love,
I want to be by your side,
today, tomorrow, and after
until the last day of our lives.

# *The Raindrop*

Rain, rain and more rain, as if it was never going to end. It is like a life concert from heaven, as if Nature were the composer of such music. It was a melody with many variations, from soft to very loud, from allegros to adagios. At moments, the wind accompanied the music, shaking the branches of the trees or moving as whips hitting the earth on its way... It was scary at times, especially when it came with thunder and lightning, and calming at others

It was a very dark night. A new moon is taking her time for her makeover, so she can show her shinning face a few days from now. She is getting ready for her last appearance of this year.

A new day has arrived. The showers continue falling non-stop.

The windows usually clean and dry were decorated with transparent drops of water making moving mosaics, hypnotically addictive. I watched as they made their way down, sliding on the surface of the glass. One drop, a very small one, was suspended, waiting for its turn to fall. She contemplated her surroundings as if having to make a decision she was not equipped to make. It seemed as if she were asking: "Should I partner with another drop and hold each other with a big warm hug, melting our individuality for the common good, or should I continue my natural way alone?"

The two drops discussed their points of view, over and over again, as if time did not exist. There were very good arguments in favour of being together..., other arguments were more inclined to their own independence.

They were not able to decide.

The sun started showing its face.

The drops dried on their spots.

The cleaning lady whipped them off.

# *Spanish Stories*

# *Cositas*

El tiempo pasa, y no en vano. Muestra su marca en las arruguitas, el pelo plateado, el paso lento, la visión borrosa, la excusa de "escuchar selectivamente" cuando en realidad ya no se oye tan claro como antes y hay que pedir repeticiones diplomáticamente. Las partes del cuerpo creadas para durar cierto tiempo empiezan a ser reemplazadas, los dientes, las rodillas, las caderas..., y la memoria, ayudada con fotos, cartas y tarjetas escritas con mano firme, música y canciones que nos hacen vibrar de emoción o de tristeza, los olores impregnados, los sentidos activados.

Envejecer no es fácil. Mirando atrás me doy cuenta de la vida tan privilegiada que he tenido. No me han faltado (diría más bien que me han sobrado) las cosas básicas, el amor de mi framilia (familia y amigos), educación, viajes... y cada día me doy cuenta de lo poco que necesito para vivir una vida con calidad. Cositas que creía imprescindibles se han vuelto innecesarias, la simplicidad y el contacto con la naturaleza parece llenarme más que el ruido de los carros tocando corneta, corriendo a toda velocidad para llegar a su destino al mismo tiempo que el que va lento; el sonido de la lluvia y de los pájaros son más melódicos que oír las noticias en la radio, casi siempre negativas, crímenes, guerras, casos de corrupción, inmigrantes muriendo tratando de llegar a puertos seguros; un buen libro para leer siempre es mucho mejor que los programas de televisión que te hipnotizan y que no puedes perderte; una sonrisa, una mirada, un abrazo cálido, un chiste, un sueño...

...y hoy leo la noticia de alguien famoso que ha partido, y siento como si hubiese sido un familiar cercano. Lo lloro, lo recuerdo, lo extraño como mío..., como me ha pasado con actores, músicos, Mandela, Kennedy, Robin Williams, Steve Jobs, Wayne Dyer...Gente que han dejado estela, que partieron dejando una huella, un camino, un ejemplo, que creyeron en su causa, que dejaron su mundo un poquito mejor que como lo encontraron, o por lo menos eso es lo que quisieron...

Dejemos la casa, el mundo de nuestros coterráneos, mejor de como la encontramos, aunque sea "un poquito mejor". Que nuestra vida haya valido la pena, que nuestras palabras hayan querido ser escuchadas, que nuestros errores nos hayan permitido aprender, que nuestro ejemplo sea inspiración.

# *Sin Previo Aviso*

Alberto se encontraba trabajando para una empresa. Nunca faltaba al trabajo. Siempre llegaba puntual y bien acicalado, y cumplía con todo lo que se le pedía. En casa era igual. Siempre listo, como los scouts, para lo que fuera necesario. Los niños asistían a una escuela privada. La mamá los llevaba todos los días, lonchera en mano, con las tareas revisadas. Tomaban vacaciones una vez al año. También iban los fines de semana a la playa, o de paseo a la montaña, a montar bicicleta, a visitar a los familiares y amigos. Daba la impresión de que todo estaba en orden.

Un día, saliendo de su casa como de costumbre, y sin previo aviso, lo estaban esperando en la calle. Ni tiempo le dio de reaccionar. Le pusieron un pañuelo encima de la nariz y la boca, y lo montaron en una camioneta con rumbo desconocido. Unos vecinos grabaron el terrible suceso con sus cámaras de video. Corrieron a casa de la vecina con la noticia.

Al recibirla, Anita se quedó paralizada. Los niños no entendían lo que ocurría. El mundo parecía haberse esfumado y, de repente, no había fondo donde plantarse. Todo daba vueltas, todo era confuso, todo se sentía perdido.

Unas horas más tarde llegaba la primera llamada telefónica. Exigencias, órdenes, amenazas, palabras cortas sin sentido pero cargadas de rencor. Venían de no sé dónde. Cada vez más confundida, sin saber qué hacer. Con el dinero de los sueldos apenas alcanzaba para vivir, y ahora esto...El dinero no era lo más importante, aunque de éste dependía que soltaran a Alberto, el padre de familia, el esposo ejemplar.

Una segunda llamada llegó, pero esta vez venía de una institución del Estado. Con el mismo tono malandro, no sólo volvían a pedir más dinero, sino que se escuchaban los gritos de Alberto mientras lo torturaban. De camino a su calabozo, y mientras estaba bajo las drogas inhaladas, le habían colocado un cinturón con explosivos, y ahora estaba siendo acusado de terrorismo. Eran tácticas que se habían convertido en rutina, en un país sin ley.

Pasaron muchos días en silencio.

La angustia carcomía a la familia. Los niños fueron enviados a casa de una tía que vivía en el exterior. Un asilo político se había otorgado en tiempo record.

El teléfono paró de sonar.

Ana recorrió todas las cárceles, todas las estaciones de policía, todos los hospitales, todos los tribunales, y todos los días regresaba a casa sin respuestas. Su alma llena sólo de recuerdos, se vaciaba de esperanza. Cerraba los ojos para descansar, pero sólo lograba escuchar los llamados desesperados.

Envejeció pronto. Su tristeza la acompañó, también sin previo aviso, prematuramente, hasta su última morada.

Alberto finalmente fue puesto en libertad, pero ya no encontró ni a su mujer, ni a sus hijos. Estaba sólo. Le habían quitado la vida en vida.

# *Curiosidad*

Hambre de conocimientos, sed de sabiduría,
Nunca satisfechos con el día a día.
La curiosidad mató al gato,
dice por ahí la vida
Pero yo prefiero ser curiosa a morir siempre aburrida.

"Sólo sé que no sé nada",
dijo Platón años atrás,
cuando aún ni existían
computadoras, páginas Web, videojuegos y demás.

No es solo conocer las letras,
Hay millones de cosas más,
viajar por la vida es aventura sin igual...
conocer nuevos sitios, nuevas gentes, culturas de allá
solo puede enriquecernos con lo que no nos pueden quitar.

La inversión vale la pena,
Me refiero a las ganas y voluntad,
Y se adapta a todos los bolsillos si ubicada tu mente está,
Así que ya no hay excusa que valga si te quieres educar.

## *Mi Mejor Momento*

El mejor momento del día es cuando abro los ojos en la mañana y doy gracias por un día más en este mundo. Me estiro después de haber estado torcida toda la noche para no despertar a la felina que me hace compañía y que duerme a sus anchas sin importarle cuánto espacio ocupa, luego le abro la puerta a Lady Gata para que salga a hacer su ronda matutina después de haber dormido tan plácida....y si, ella también ronca, bajito...

Me levanto y preparo mi cafecito. Ése no puede fallar. Lo disfruto lentamente. Me acompañan los primeros sonidos de la mañana, los pájaros parece que vinieran a saludar.

Hace unos días hablaba con una amiga por teléfono. Al fondo escuché ruidos. Le pregunté qué eran y me contestó con una carcajada...jeje, ya te olvidaste de los sonidos de la gran ciudad? La verdad que sí. Mis ruidos suenan más a música. Las ramas de los árboles parecen bailar al ritmo del viento, las olas del mar vienen y van, a veces suaves, a veces malhumoradas como si hubieran pasado la noche de parranda. La lluvia cae, refresca, y luego se despide para ir a otro lugar.

Preparo mi plan, qué tengo que hacer hoy? No, no, no...se me había olvidado. He cambiado el verbo "tengo que" por "Quiero". No siento mis quehaceres como obligaciones, cumplo con ellos porque quiero, porque tienen una razón de ser. Cuando no la encuentro, la busco. Si se me hace pesada, pienso en su beneficio. Confieso que a veces no me provoca...y confieso también que ya no me siento la magnánima que todo lo puede. Soy tan vulnerable como tú, soy débil y soy fuerte.

Sigo con mi mejor momento del día, después de algunas horas. Todos los días diferentes, todos los días con retos, con alegrías y con lágrimas cuando hablo de mi patria bonita. En esos momentos, el corazón se me pone como una pasita, los ojos aguados, y la piel me tiembla con una emoción de angustia, de tristeza, de melancolía y hasta de irracionalidad. Mi bella Venezuela, estás perdida, pero te vamos a encontrar, te vamos a rescatar, te vamos a cuidar y no te vamos a dejar ir más. Te creíste el cuento y seguiste, inocente, a quienes te lo estaban echando, y caíste en la trampa. Aguanta, ya vamos a tu rescate.

Mi mejor momento es cuando cuento cuentos, cuando transmito. Busco la oportunidad para ser un libro viviente, para ser una voz que se escuche, con mis historias y las historias de mi pueblo.

Mi mejor momento de la noche, es cuando, después de cenar, me acuesto en mi hamaca, con la música de Simón Díaz, de Juan Vicente Torrealba, de María Teresa Chacín (ya los pajaritos están durmiendo), y sueño despierta con mis recuerdos, con mi familia, con mis amigos, con las playas, las montañas, los llanos, con mi gente linda, con mis profesores y hasta con los novios que me aguantaron y que me quisieron montón.

Mi mejor momento es cualquier momento en que respiro, en que puedo ver, escuchar, tocar, cantar, escribir, pensar. Mi mejor momento es cuando estoy sola y cuando estoy acompañada. Mi mejor momento es...

# *Autoestima*

Muere antes de nacer, cae antes de volar,
se esconde antes de salir, el miedo inunda el lugar.
Paralizado observo y no me atrevo a mostrar
los dones que llevo por dentro, el miedo me vuelve a
inundar.
Solo en el mundo me encuentro, refugiado en cualquier
lugar,
de repente suena el teléfono, tiemblo antes de contestar,
son sólo buenas noticias, son las que quiero escuchar.
Me siento como luna llena que saliendo anda ya,
la persigo para verla, recatada parece estar.
Ella sabe que es muy linda, se lo dicen de verdad
pero hoy no sé lo que pasa que no desea brotar.
Me muevo de un lado al otro para poderla alcanzar,
parece que tiene pena, parece que quiere jugar.
Me guiña detrás de los pinos, después no la veo más,
su jornada ha terminado, ya se fue a descansar.
La mía apenas comienza, salgo de mi malestar
a enfrentar nuevos retos, a vivir con libertad.

# *La Ropa*

La plancha me mira desde lejos como queriendo decirme que la he olvidado...y tiene razón. No la he acariciado en muchos meses, no la he usado para estirar la ropa que se arrugará apenas me la ponga. En el campo ni las vacas, ni los gatos me preguntan por qué no plancho...Frente a mi ventana los mininos se entienden entre ellos y se muerden las colas, revolotean, corren, contentos y despreocupados.

He cambiado mis hábitos ligeramente. Si voy a la ciudad, dejo que el vapor en el baño juegue con las fibras de las telas...De todas formas hace frío y llueve, y aunque me ocupe de planchar, igual tendré que ponerme mi poncho, planchado permanente, calentico, cómodo. Mientras escribo, recuerdo el día de ayer. El sendero protegido por los árboles por donde se filtra el tímido sol, formando túneles disfrutados por miles de años, por diferentes gentes. Quisiera que me hablaran y me contaran... Caminamos por las ruinas de un castillo al lado de un hermoso y claro riachuelo, el agua jugando, saltando, moviendo las piedras como queriendo oír su propia música. Las sobrevivientes rocas han sido testigos de tanto, y quisiera que me hablaran y me contaran... El viento, soplando, acariciando mi cara, me dice tanto, y dice nada. ...y pasa un día más. La página en blanco de mi diario está llena, parece que no le cabe una letra más...pero hay tanto que escribir, hay tanto que contar. Cada día diferente. Pido prestada otra página para continuar. No quiero dejarlas en blanco. Las lleno con la mano firme en el teclado o con la mano temblorosa en el papel, con los recuerdos del día y del nuevo amanecer. Y como la plancha, la pluma se vuelve otra extraña que no quiero dejar atrás. Prefiero escribir con ella, mandar cartas y tarjetas hechas a mano, leer las hojas de los libros impresos, escuchar las canciones de antes. Nostalgia, melancolía. Por momentos... vivo en el pasado, pero mi presente es lo que ahora tengo, es mi realidad, y no la quiero perder.

# *La Clase Da Hoy*

Llego corriendo a casa, tras haber pasado la mañana en el mejor salón de clases. No llevé libros, ni cuadernos... sólo mi mente abierta, como se hacía hace muchos años. Mi maestro no es Simón Rodríguez, ni Platón, ni Aristóteles. Mi maestro de hoy es un manzano, un árbol cargado de frutas verdes y rojas. Los cuervos han tocado el timbre anunciando que ya algunas han madurado y que es tiempo de cosecharlas.

Decido atender al llamado.

Con mis manos un poco callosas y curtidas por el tiempo, y sin prisas, voy acariciando cada una. La que está lista vibra de una manera especial, como diciéndome que no la deje caer. Se desprende entonces generosa, y le doy gracias. No espera nada a cambio, no tengo que pagar por ella. Mi retribución es darle su valor, es honrarla por sus esfuerzos, es compartirla, es comerla. Me pongo a pensar que la naturaleza es la única que ha cuidado de ese manzano. La lluvia, el sol, el viento....sin químicos ni fertilizantes, lo han hecho un árbol fuerte. Sus ramas sirven de columpio a los pájaros, su sombra protege al caminante, sus hojas secas regenerarán la tierra donde las raíces han decidido hacer su hogar. ...y me asombro de nuevo ante tanta belleza, ...y aprendo sobre el ritmo de la naturaleza en todo; en los árboles que nos dan sus frutos, no todos al mismo tiempo, en la planta que nos da sus flores, en la oruga que se convertirá en mariposa, en la niña que se transforma en mujer. Todo a su tiempo, no hay que forzar la marcha. Cada planta es diferente, cada cual madura cuando las condiciones se dan. Si recojo las manzanas antes de su momento óptimo, serán ácidas y no las podré comer. Se perderán. Si quiero que la oruga salga volando, no lo podrá hacer. Si empujo a la niña a que sea mujer antes de su tiempo, también envejecerá antes. El curso para cada quien es diferente. ¿Cuál es la prisa, entonces? Tómate tu tiempo, el que sea necesario.

# *La Pelota Azul*

En un banco me senté a leer. Levanto la vista al ver pasar a los que pasean con sus perros, con sus niños, a los que van solos, a los que trotan, a los que van lento. Algunos saludan, otros simplemente ignoran. Las ardillas preparándose para la estación fría, van recogiendo las castañas con sus patitas delanteras...Observo. Escucho los pasos de los que pasan. El sonido del agua del río que viaja hacia otro destino diferente al que tenía hace. Se aparecen cuando menos uno se los espera. Impredecibles. No sé si es el paso de los años que hace esos momentos de dicha más frecuentes, o es que siempre estuvieron allí y con la prisa del diario vivir no podía reconocerlos. Es una plenitud absolutamente distinta, es alegría combinada con serenidad. Es como una nueva energía que llena y que quieres compartir, y que no quieres que se te escape. Ya no le busco la explicación a todo porque he aprendido que mucho no la tiene. Ya no pierdo mi valioso tiempo cuestionando misterios de fe. ¿Por qué el sol está brillando hoy, y no ayer? ¿Por qué, por qué...? A veces sin respuestas. Hoy estoy viva, ¡hoy vivo!

# *La Cola*

Je Je...¡Dame la cola!

Cuando usé esa expresión frente a unos colegas profesores de otras tierras, se me quedaron mirando como diciendo... qué pasada, qué atrevida. Para mí, esa expresión, en ese momento, sólo significaba una cosa...No tenía carro y necesitaba que alguien me acercara a cierto lugar.

Se me quedó la espinita clavada, y quise averiguar más sobre el uso de la palabra. Para mi sorpresa, encontré muchos más usos de los que esperaba.

Una de las definiciones tiene que ver con lo que se cultiva...así vinícola, las uvas, frutícola, frutas, agrícola, que tiene que ver con el agro... También se usa para indicar que somos habitantes de la tierra...soy terrícola, cavernícola. La cola es la extremidad final de la columna vertebral, que puede ser larga o corta. Gracias a Dios, la costumbre de cortarla a los perros por razones netamente estéticas está cayendo en desuso. Mover la cola indica momentos emocionales, de alegrías o de miedos... sirven de abanico en temporadas de calor, y de juego cuando los gatos tratan de alcanzar las suyas propias. La cola, es lo opuesto a la cabeza. Estar a la cola de algo es estar al final. La cola del cometa que vuela lo hace distinguido, lo define. Tener cola de paja, remordimientos... Cola de caballo, media cola...estilos de peinados prácticos, cuando no se tiene mucho tiempo para otros... Ponerle la cola al burro...en nuestras fiestas infantiles. Muchas veces la cola aparecía al lado de un ojo, de la oreja...en fin, muy divertido. La cola de pegar... Dame una cola, una colita...aquellas bebidas llenas de azúcar que aún se encuentran en algunos abastos. Las colas en el tráfico, a veces "eternas", de minutos y hasta de horas...se han vuelto tan peligrosas! Las colas para entrar al cine, para pagar las cuentas, para ser atendido en los hospitales, para comprar comida y medicinas. Colas para sacarse el pasaporte o la cédula, para buscar algo en los tribunales, para agarrar el metro, para entrar y salir del país... Colas para votar... pero lo más importante de las colas, es que dejaremos de ser la cola del ratón, ratones que viven entre la basura, para volver a ser cabeza de león, con la cabeza en alto, con el orgullo presente que nos ayudará a recuperar a nuestra bella patria, Venezuela, la de las siete estrellas...sin cola!

# *La Pieza Que Faltaba*

Existía en un lejano país una zona muy especial, con montañas mágicas, con un río que cantaba a su paso por las rocas como si las acariciara con su voz, con pajaritos jugando en el aire, con árboles cargados de historias... En medio de ese país, una granja hermosa, donde vivía un granjero solitario. El granjero, un hombre de gran corazón, generoso hasta el extremo, había hecho de su lugar una especie de paraíso. Sin embargo, el granjero no era feliz. Parecía como si caminara con una nube gris sobre su cabeza que lo cubría de una sombra en forma de telaraña, que dejaba pasar tímida los rayos del sol. Un día, una de sus nietas, una niña linda con el pelo con rubios rulitos naturales, a quien le gustaban mucho armar rompecabezas, le trajo un regalo al abuelo. Era un rompecabezas especialmente hecho para él. Lo pusieron sobre una gran mesa de madera y comenzaron juntos a armarlo. Varias semanas pasaron hasta que, al casi terminarlo, se dieron cuenta que faltaba una pieza muy importante. De pronto, Opa se dio cuenta de que el rompecabezas era su propia granja, con todo lo que había en ella: los tractores, las flores, los gatos...hasta su propia imagen con la nube que lo acompañaba. Buscaron la pieza por todas partes, en la caja, debajo de los muebles, en los sitios menos esperados, pero la pieza no aparecía. Mientras tanto, en un pueblo cercano, una maestra jubilada había abierto una tienda de rompecabezas. La maestra era una mujer inteligente y cariñosa, a quien le gustaban muchas cosas: los animales, la naturaleza, cantar y cocinar. En su tienda siempre tenía bizcochitos hechos por ella, lo que atraía a los niños del lugar, para quienes había preparado una mesa donde armaban rompecabezas. Una caja especial contenía piezas sueltas perdidas, que buscaban acomodo. Ella cantaba, era feliz en su propio mundo. Opa y su nieta fueron de compras y pasaron delante de la tienda. La curiosidad hizo que entraran a preguntar por la pieza faltante del rompecabezas que tenían en casa. La mujer les señaló la caja de piezas perdidas, y como cosa extraña, una pieza saltarina se posó en la mano del granjero. Sorprendido, se la llevó a casa. La pieza, con la cara de una mujer que le resultó familiar, encajaba perfectamente. Había terminado de armar el rompecabezas. Celebró con la nieta. De repente se dieron cuenta que el rompecabezas cobraba vida, los personajes hablaban, los pájaros volaban, el río pasaba juguetón. La cara de la mujer era la cara de la dueña de la tienda. Sin pensarlo, y con la pieza en mano, se fueron hasta allá, la compararon, la maestra sonrió. Era ella, la que faltaba. Opa la tomó de la mano, y sin decir palabra, la llevó a su nuevo hogar. La nube desapareció, y los colores grises y oscuros se iluminaron como por arte de magia.

## *Colorilandia*

Había una vez un país rodeado de arcoíris, fenómeno único en el mundo. Los arcoíris iluminaban los espacios con luz cuando ésta era necesaria, pero también emitían música individualizada para cada habitante de acuerso a sus gustos personales, que no interfería o molestaba a los demás. La gente cantaba y bailaba, y era feliz. Las comidas preferidas eran producidas siguiendo los deseos y necesidades de cada quien. De noche, una suave brisa cargada con olores relajantes acompañaba los sueños

Un día, siete colorilandeses, atraídos por la curiosidad, decidieron emprender un viaje camino al horizonte, donde creían que nacían los arcoíris. Prepararon entonces sus mochilas y prometieron al gobernador que regresarían con muchas respuestas.

Entonces empezaron a caminar...

Los meses se nombrarían a medida que fueran pasando y dependiendo del element o la actividad más importante del momento. Los nombres de los meses nunca se repetían y la cantidad de días variaría de acuerdo a la capacidad de adaptación de los siete aventureros. Los meses cambiaban cuando alguno de ellos decidiera ala hazaña.

Así, el primer mes de la travesía fue Solegust. El sol brillaba intensamente, y durante todo el día. No habían noches. La piel quemaba, los ojos ardían. No había sombra por ningún lado. El calor era insoportable. Uno de los caminantes sufrió un shock de calor, y decidió regresar a Colorilandia, donde los días eran frescos y agradables...y contó la historia.

A consecuencia del mes anterior, se produjeron incendios espontáneos que fueron destruyendo bosques y montañas. El Segundo mes fue nombrado Ardoroso. Todo ardía. Los seis amigos se la pasaban apagando las llamas y creando cortafuegos. Sudaban, se deshidrataban y ya ni descansaban. Otro de los aliados decidió regresar a casa...y contó la historia.

Llegó entonces el mes Tormentero, el mes de las tormentas interminables. Los truenos sonaban tan duro que los caminantes tenían que taparse los oídos. Los relámpagos, cargados de electricidad, los hacían temblar a cada paso como si se tratara de cortocircuitos. La lluvia caía sin cesar y los caminos inundados y embarrados dificultaban el andar. Los compañeros estaban siempre mojados. Entonces, otro regresó...y contó la historia.

Lunaza comenzó. Los días eran oscuros. A veces aparecía una luna tímida, pero la mayor parte del tiempo estaba escondida entre tinieblas. Los compañeros tropezaban constantemente, se caían, se golpeaban, se torcían los pies. No podían ver el camino. Las noches se hicieron cada vez más largas. Uno más regresó...y contó la historia.

Ya solo quedaban tres coloricenses enfrentándose a los retos de cada día. Estaban tan cansados que ya ni hablaban entre ellos. Andaban siempre de muy mal humor.

La siguiente sorpresa fur Arenembre. La arena volaba fina, cubriendo los cuerpos de los tres hambrientos caminantes. No encontraban qué comer. Tragaban el polvo Amarillo, se les llenaban los oídos y las fosas nasales tapadas impedían el paso del aire y sentían ahogarse. La ropa picaba. No había manera de sacudirse porque apenas lo intentaban la arena se reproducía. Todo se complicaba. El quinto decidió regresar…y contó la historia.

Los dos restantes continuaron.

El frío extremo llegó en el mes Tiritante. Se resbalaban en el hielo, se hundían en la nieve. Los deditos de los pies se les congelaron, y les dolían. Las narices, rojas al principio, comenzaron a sangrar y se tornaron de color violeta. Casi casi estaban anestesiados con riesgo de necrosis. Entonces uno de ellos decidió regresar…y contó la historia.

El único restante, el séptimo y el más orgulloso de todos, decidió seguir su camino solo. Y en silencio absoluto. No tenia con quien hablar. No se oía nada, ni el viento, ni los animales, ni nada de nada, como si todo estuviese vacío. Era el mes Soledada. Parecía como si el tiempo se hubiese detenido. Ya nada importaba. Todo estaba ausente. El horizonte era incoloro, los arcoíris habían desaparecido.

Poco a poco, y con el paso cansado, regresó él también a Colorilandia.

Todo el pueblo y sus seis compañeros lo recibieron con los brazos abiertos, reconociendo su audacia, tenacidad y valor. Lo había intentado todo, y ahora, humilde, reconocía que su hogar era el mejor que jamás hubiera tenido. Volvió a sentir el amor de sus seres queridos, volvió a ver los colores del arcoíris, escuchó de nuevo sus canciones favoritas, a comer rico, a dormir plácido…

…y fue feliz.

## *El Momento*

Captar el momento, como los impresionistas cuando pintan sus cuadros.

Capto el momento con palabras. Mi bosquejo, mi borrador, como todos mis escritos, está lleno de imperfecciones, pero también de magia y color. Transmito con mis palabras lo que veo y lo que imagino.

En este momento, decido caminar por el bosque. Las hojas crujen a mi paso, como música en movimiento. Cae una llovizna suave que no molesta, por el contrario, parece refrescar la mente y el espíritu, los renueva. Levanto la cara al escuchar un silbido silencioso, casi imperceptible. "Mira para acá", parece decirme. Suena y se calla, como jugando al escondite. Al ubicarlo finalmente, "ajá, te caché", camino hacia allá. Me paro entre dos árboles. Observo. Allí está ella, inspirada. Con sus minúsculas agujas de tejer va construyendo su tela. Me invita a su clase, quiere que aprenda, quiere que vea. Así, a medida que los minutos van pasando, quedo como hipnotizada ante la obra de la artista desconocida. Su pincel son sus patitas, su pintura sale de ella misma. Estoy en primera fila. El cuadro es una malla con diseños exquisitos que pocas veces dedicamos el tiempo para verlos. Se balancea suave como una hamaca amarrada entre dos palos. Sus hilos son tan fuertes como el acero, y a la vez suaves y flexibles. De pronto la veo lanzándose en rapel hacia el vacío,...pero no se cae. Milagrosamente la veo suspendida como en una cuerda floja, como si jugara. Tenaz, sigue tejiendo, es su pasatiempo. Me pasa el tiempo. Regreso para escribir. Uno de mis pasatiempos.

Nota del autor: Las telarañas se usan para detener hemorragias, para la industria textil, chalecos antibalas, redes de pescar, medicina regenerativa, atrapar mosquitos y muchas cosas más. La naturaleza es sabia. Aprender a respetarla y a quererla sería un gran paso para la humanidad.

# *Un Nudo En La Garganta*

Mamá, mamáááá! ...gritaba en mi sueño.

El eco de mi voz parecía retumbar por todas partes. El estruendo me despertó.

Como de costumbre, miré el reloj...y como de costumbre también, eran las tres de la mañana. Sentí un nudo en la garganta. Quería gritar de nuevo, quería volverla a llamar, pero la voz no me salía. Me quedé muda, acompañada por mis pensamientos. Y sentí miedo. No, no puedo tener miedo. Tengo que ser fuerte. No es el momento de flaquear. Las lágrimas corrían sin parar, como si estuviesen compitiendo entre ellas. Seguían saliendo de mis ojos y no podía pararlas. Pasó el tiempo sin sentirlo, y me quedé dormida de nuevo. Mamá vino. Se sentó a mi lado. Me abrazó. Me consoló. Pude escucharla. Sus sabias palabras, como caricias, me dijeron suavemente: "Estaré siempre contigo, aunque no me veas. Estoy en tu corazón, llevas mi sangre. Asimismo, tus hijos y tus nietos llevan la tuya y la mía. Disfrútalos mientras tengas vida. Llámalos cuando amanezca. Diles cuánto los amas, con ese amor de madre." Ahora duerme el último pedacito...como cuando tenías que levantarte para ir a la escuela y te quedaba ese poquito en la cama. ¿Te recuerdas? El despertador sonó. La almohada aún estaba mojada. Me levanté y llamé a mis hijos.

# *Ahora, El Momento*

Hace tiempo decidí no tener cortinas y disfruto de la lluvia, del sol, de las noches estrelladas y de las nubladas. Los curiosos insectos quedan atrapados en una malla que no les permite pasar.

Cuando abrí mis ojos esta mañana una tenue luz entraba tímida, como pidiéndome permiso...o como queriendo llamar mi atención. Después de agradecer por este nuevo día, salí. Me senté en mi terracita con una taza de café. Me quedé en silencio.

Esperé...y escuché los primeros cantos de los pájaros, como si practicaran en un coro. Todos querían cantar al mismo tiempo. Las flores comienzan a abrir al mundo con sus hermosos colores. Las ramas de los árboles, con minúsculas hojitas que crecen a una velocidad casi visible como diciendo que no quieren perderse esta temporada. Las abejas, estirando sus alitas salen a volar buscando el néctar que las alimenta. Y me digo...es un nuevo amanecer, un nuevo ciclo de vida. Yo tampoco quiero perdérmelo!

# *La Gata y La Ardilla*

Era un día de primavera. El sol se asomaba tranquilo. Los pájaros se escuchaban cantar como casi todas las mañanas.

Un sonido inusual, intermitente, viene desde detrás del sofá, como si fuese uno de esos resortes oxidados. Kuik... kuik...Qué será? De pronto vi una cabecita asomarse con precaución por uno de los lados, como si estuviese calculando, pensando en su escape. Es la cabeza de una ardilla en pánico. Ya no llama por ayuda de las demás, quienes no quieren arriesgarse. Esta solita y tiene que tomar alguna decisión pronto.

La gata, quien la había invitado a jugar, ha cambiado de idea, y ahora lo que quiere es ganar el juego. La observa a la distancia, se acerca, se aleja, se hace la loca pero no pierde de vista su objetivo.

La ardilla sigue, silenciosa, detrás del sofá.

Yo le abro las puertas de la casa para que tenga más salidas, más alternativas. Trato de distraer a la gata, me la llevo al cuarto.

No quiero encontrarme con el cadáver de una ardilla en mi sala. Ella debe tomar una decisión, y pronto. Es su decisión. Tiene alternativas. Tiene oportunidades, tiene riesgos.

# *Mi Viaje Llanero*

Voy navegando, sin prisas, en mi canoa, desde Colombia hasta Venezuela por el rio Arauca. Es un paseo sin igual, pasando por los llanos llenos de una exuberante fauna que enaltece un orgullo robado de la naturaleza. A lo lejos veo unos árboles frondosos, cargados de flores gigantes. Me voy acercando, y las flores parecen tener vida. Salen volando...son garzas vestidas de blanco y rojo. Los cantos que acompañan su vuelo majestuoso junto con el de los otros pájaros multicolores llenan el ambiente con una música muy particular, inimitable. Tomo miles de fotos con el único aparato moderno que me he permitido traer, mi cámara. Los demás no hacen falta. Por ahora, solo quiero disfrutar del momento, de mi momento.

El sol calienta tanto, que hasta el agua pareciera estar lo suficientemente tibia como para preparar alguna comida. Decido no arriesgarme, aunque tengo muchas ganas de refrescarme de alguna forma. Prefiero conservar la vida que ser postre de las pirañas o de algún cocodrilo pretendiendo estar dormido a las orillas del rio.

Me dejo llevar por el agua que salta rápida entre las rocas, y descansa. Parece que debe recargarse de energía antes de seguir su trayecto. No tiene itinerario, pero sabe que debe llegar a su destino.

El "oasis llanero" se presenta, invitándome a pasar la tarde en él. Lleno de palmas, de morichales. Decido amarrar mi canoa en una de esas palmeras y respirar el aire fresco en su cobijo. Ya está cayendo la tarde. El sol, cual esfera majestuosa, parece pintar el escenario de rojos, anaranjados y amarillos anunciando la despedida de su día de trabajo, para dar paso a la luna llena que iluminará la noche con esa claridad que parece la luz del estadio, allá donde juegan béisbol.

Mi canoa se mece como si fuese una hamaca, y me duermo con su vaivén...y sueño. Sueño en colores y en blanco y negro, sueño en mi idioma, sueño en mi tierra. Sueño con la gente que quiero, con los que están y con los que se han ido.

Una lluvia suave me despierta y me doy cuenta que una araña ha compartido la noche. Me muevo lenta para no asustarla, hasta que puedo deslizarme y salir de su dominio. Nos despedimos, no de la mejor manera, y sigo.

De pronto me veo acompañado de unos delfines rosados, toninas, saltando a mi pasar, pareciera como si me dieran la bienvenida al Orinoco, el río que parece mar, que ha inspirado a poetas, a cantantes, a los enamorados que se le acercan. Sus olas brillan con chispas parecidas a los cortocircuitos, similares a las chispas pasajeras en nuestros corazones cuando alguien te mira bonito.

El puente de Angostura, que me recuerda al discurso de Simón Bolívar (1819): "Muchas naciones antiguas y modernas han sacudido la opresión; pero son rarísimas las que han sabido gozar algunos preciosos momentos de libertad; muy luego han recaído en sus antiguos vicios políticos; porque son los pueblos más bien que los gobiernos los que arrastran tras sí la tiranía. El hábito de la dominación los hace insensibles a los encantos del honor y de la prosperidad nacional; y miran con indolencia la gloria de vivir en el movimiento de la libertad, bajo la tutela de leyes dictadas por su propia voluntad".

Me sacuden sus palabras y me hacen volver a la realidad. Ya estoy por llegar al mar, al final de mi camino.

# *Ahora*

Un tiempo para mi
se siente y se dice raro, pero es así
¿Cuándo fue la última vez que lo hice así?
¿Cuándo fue la última vez que tú lo hiciste así?
Mi supervisora me preguntó y no supe contestar,
pero me dio pie para consciente analizar que el tiempo
pasa y que no vuelve atrás
Y ¿qué he hecho hoy por mí, y qué por mi bienestar?
Si bien es cierto que pensar y ayudar a otros nutre
mi espíritu,
otras cosas descubro ahora también lo llenan,
y camino clara, sin egoísmos ni reproches,
a cubrirme de tu esencia, de tu naturaleza,
de la vida misma, de las noches y los días.
Vivo la lluvia, vivo las sombras, la brisa,
el sol, y las nubes que me ayudan a imaginar
historias detrás de ellas que solíamos contar
cuando éramos niñas jugando en el carro
cuando en familia acostumbrábamos viajar
por los llanos y las montañas, las selvas y desiertos,
y por las hermosas playas de mi Venezuela natal.

## *Si Yo Fuese*

Si yo fuese un caballo, me gustaría tener su nobleza, su fortaleza y su dulzura.

Si yo fuese un delfín, me gustaría recorrer los mares, saltar con energía y alegría las olas y brillar con esa piel de seda.

Si yo fuese una vaca, me gustaría ser una "vaca feliz", caminando todo el dia por praderas llenas de rico pasto.

Si yo fuese un ave, me gustaría ser el águila que extiende sus alas, dejándose acariciar por el viento, viajando magnánima, imponente.

Si yo fuese un perro, me gustaría ser atlético, tierno, confiable, leal.

Si yo fuese un gato, me gustaría ser curioso...con precaución.

Si yo fuese un insecto, me gustaría ser una abeja que entrega su vida por un mejor mundo.

Si yo fuese una flor, me gustaría ser una rosa amarilla, que inunde el ambiente con su aroma, y con su luz ilumine el camino de quien esté perdido.

...pero como no soy ninguno de ellos, quisiera aprender de cada uno y ser un ser humano noble, fuerte, dulce, libre, astuto, leal, atlético, confiable, inteligente, alegre, energético, tierno, con orgullo y humildad, tal como los animales que adoro y admiro, como las plantas generosas que nos regalan sus flores y sus frutos, como las montañas y los mares, como el cielo, la lluvia, el sol, la luna y las estrellas.

# *Entre Ficción y Realidad*

Entre ficción y realidad unas vienen y otras van,
a veces me siento cual testigo, otras veces, protagonista principal
¿Cuándo cruzar la línea?
Me pregunto una vez más,

y pongo mis sueños en la bolsa que pronto podré vaciar
en una tierra nueva que con brazos abiertos está ya
Para recibirme pronto en ella y volverlos realidad.

# *El Duende*

Caminando entre los árboles de eucaliptus, bajo la incesante lluvia que refresca el ambiente con el aroma característico que llega al punto de remover algunos recuerdos de otros tiempos. Me paro. Respiro con los brazos abiertos de par en par como queriendo purificar mis pulmones y sacar tanto polvo acumulado por la (in) evitable contaminación del progreso.

Me resbalo, caigo sentada sobre una roca vestida de musgo, y decido descansar un rato. Mis sentidos se renuevan.

De repente oigo pasitos sobre las hojas mojadas que están detrás de mí. Volteo. Me sorprendo al ver un duendecito real (hasta ese momento pensaba que no existían). Se presenta. Ito es su nombre. Me pregunta el mío y entramos en franca conversación. Me observa y yo lo observo, atónita, sin saber qué decir.

Hablando de todo y de nada, como si nos conociéramos de siempre, me dice que observe las montañas que tenemos delante. Llevan el lomo doblado por el peso de los árboles que cargan en sus espaldas. No se quejan. Sienten el cosquilleo de las raíces entrelazadas en su interior, los masajes de las ramas que se mueven al ritmo de la brisa. Las montañas, a cambio, les ofrecen sustento, un hogar que pareciera ser seguro. Se benefician mutuamente.

Al oeste observamos otra montaña. No sé si se ve oscura porque está pasando una nube gris…, pero Ito, mi nuevo amigo, me dice que esa no es la razón. La montaña está de luto porque sus árboles se quemaron el año pasado en uno de esos incendios forestales. La dejaron desnuda, o mejor dicho, vestida de cenizas que se lleva el viento a su paso. Está triste. Ha perdido su carga que era su razón de ser, su orgullo.

Cierro los ojos. Me duermo.

No sé cuánto tiempo pasó.

Encuentro una nota escrita en inmaculada caligrafía junto a un trébol de cuatro hojas.

Recuerda, dice, que tener lo suficiente es más que suficiente. No cargues más de lo que puedas o tu espalda se doblará. No es necesario. Viaja liviana, con el cosquilleo de tus recuerdos, con el verdor de las montañas, con el azul del mar, con las sombras dejadas por el viento.

Dejo mi mochila. Me voy con lo esencial.

Mi camino continúa…1en paz.

## *Fusa y La Patinadora*

Hoy es un día especial..., mejor dicho, OTRO día especial, como cada uno que pasa.

Mi gata Fusa trajo a casa por primera vez el fruto de sus continuos esfuerzos de infinita paciencia cuando se queda observando algo que se mueve. La he visto saltar sobre insectos y pájaros varias veces sin resultados satisfactorios para ella. Pero hoy tiene cara de satisfacción. Logró su primer premio; un ratoncito que no tuvo la buena suerte de escapar ileso. Recompensada finalmente lo disfruta en el patio.

Me recuerda la historia de Natalia, quien me contó un día que había sido seleccionada por sus habilidades atléticas para formar parte del equipo local infantil de patinaje sobre hielo. No sólo era un honor, pero también un privilegio. Ella no entendía lo que todo eso significaba, ya que apenas tenía seis añitos. Ella sólo sabía que, mientras sus compañeritos de clase iban a jugar después de la escuela, ella tenía que ir a practicar su patinaje, a entrenar por horas bajo la estricta supervisión de su entrenador que pareciera no haber tenido niñez. Le gritaba, le hacía repetir las piruetas una y otra vez aunque estuviese agotada, y hasta contaba con el apoyo patriótico de mis padres cuando me levantaba una vara de bambú de forma amenazante. Natalia obedecía, no tenía otra opción. Llena de moretones llegaba a su casa todas las noches a hacer los deberes escolares y a veces se quedaba dormida sobre los cuadernos. El cansancio era tal que ya ni pensaba.

Pasaron los años…

Natalia se sentía sola. Su niñez había sido corta. Su destino había sido comprometido por sus padres y su entrenador.

Su momento llegó cuando la llamaron para las competencias, esta vez, a nivel nacional. Era la primera vez en la historia que su aldea iba a ser representada. Soñaba con la música, con las rutinas. La costurera preparó su ropero, coordinando de manera excepcional con las melodías que iba a bailar. La prensa la vino a entrevistar. Nunca antes le habían tomado tantas fotos.

El dia tan esperado había llegado. Sus padres y su entrenador la acompañaron. Los maestros y sus compañeros de escuela, los vecinos...todos, todos estaban pegados del televisor, y Natalia, encargada de representarlos. Sentía que no podía, que no debía fracasar.

Sudaba esperando su turno para pasar a la pista. Temblaba como gelatina. Respiraba, transpiraba. De pronto escuchó su nombre y salió confiada: la música y la danza comenzaron al unísono. Parecía como si volara como los pájaros, flotaba ligera como las nubes, sonreía, estaba transportada por la emoción del momento. Y de pronto, al hacer el triple salto que tanto y tanto había practicado, resbaló y cayó. Se levantó de inmediato y pudo terminar su presentación con el poquito orgullo que le quedaba, y con la carita llena de lágrimas que corrían, escapando de sus ojitos tristes.

Tenía que ser fuerte.

"La victoria tiene un centenar de padres, pero la derrota es huérfana" (JFK).

El rechazo y el reclamo en la cara de la gente la hizo reflexionar.

Las lecciones y los sacrificios de tantas horas y horas de práctica no podían haber sido en vano. Así que, como en la pista, se levantó de nuevo. Esta vez, su entrenador le dio la espalda y la abandonó. Sus padres, al sentirse humillados por el fracaso, también la abandonaron. Siguió sola, con la música y las rutinas que ella había escogido y creado, las que le salían del alma. Se inscribió en las competencias nacionales y fue escalando los peldaños del éxito poco a poco. Representó a su país en las Olimpiadas y hasta trajo de vuelta la añorada medalla de oro.

La historia de Natalia, paralela a la de la gatita Fusa, son solo semejantes a las que vivimos diariamente. Estudiamos, observamos, practicamos, caemos. La diferencia está en que ellas se levantaron y siguieron adelante. No fue fácil, el precio pagado fue alto, pero la perseverancia, la tenacidad y la autoestima se vieron recompensadas con un ratoncito y una medalla de oro.

# *Chocolate Caliente*

AmanecAmaneció muy frío. Las temperaturas bajaron durante la noche. Me provoca quedarme acurrucada entre las cobijas, pero tengo que abrirle la puerta a la perrita y a la gata para que salgan...rapidito. Ellas también prefieren el calor del hogar.

Bueno, ya me levanté. Doy gracias por este nuevo día.

Camino a la cocina y decido prepararme una taza de chocolate caliente.

Escojo la taza que me regalaron hace muchos años. Es una taza de cerámica, color tierra, sin pintar, y puedo, en mi imaginación, ver al artesano escogiendo el barro, moldeándolo con paciencia, como cada pieza única que hace. Tiene el sabor de allá.

Ya la olla está lista y el chocolate espeso listo para ser servido. Acaricio la taza que ya está llena con el sabroso líquido y me caliento las manos. Pienso. El último chocolate que me tomé fue en Galicia, al terminar mi Camino a Santiago. Uno de los mejores que me he tomado. Espeso. Los churros se hundían con dificultad y salían bañados, marrones, invitándome para que los comiera.

También pienso en los pudines de chocolate que preparaban en casa. Las hermanas nos peleábamos para raspar la olla una vez que la habían vaciado en unos cacharritos individuales de vidrio. Los recuerdos me llevan, me llenan, me distraen...

De repente, la perrita ladra. Ella también quiere su desayuno.

# *Insomnio*

No, no sufro de ése, pero anoche no podía dormir,
mientras la cabeza me daba vueltas a mil por mil
y pensé en las personas que de verdad están en ese vaivén
de su mente en sus almohadas, al descansar.
Ponerse en los zapatos del otro no siempre fácil es,
pero al pasarlo en carne propia es posible comprender
las penas y atabares de otros, en éste y otro quehacer
del que uno se cree inmune, de que nunca me tocará, pero
tarde o temprano tendré.
Con tantas cosas pendientes no sé ni por dónde empezar
o continuar, mejor dicho, con tanto arreglar y botar.
Simplificar mi vida de tanta cosa acumulá
y dejar espacio libre para nuevas experiencias arribar,
No es tarea fácil y parece también la de nunca acabar,
ojala varita mágica tuviera, solucionando todo con un
simple "zas"
Entre cajas y peroles, entre papeles y más
cuánta cosa guarda uno, cuántas memorias, de atrás,
de alegrías y penas, de logros, de fracasos, de amores,
de viajes, de estudios, de parrandas y alborotás,
Y me pregunto...de remordimientos? Y haciendo un
llamado a mi humildad
reconozco que si tengo algunos, y el momento
ha llegado ya
para pedir disculpas a quienes daño hice sin querer

queriendo, y siempre sin voluntad,
por inmadurez, por orgullo, y a veces hasta por necesidad,
Herí a algunos, me herí yo mucho más,
pero aprendí las lecciones que hoy me hacen vivir
agradecida a no poder más.
Seguir adelante nos queda solo mirando hacia atrás
Para coger el impulso y referencia, para dar un poco más,
para compartir las bendiciones de las que muy contenta
está,
ésta que escribe sin rima, sin contar silabas, sin pensar
sólo lo que le viene a la mente en este momento real.

## *Cuando Sabes…*

Caminaba por el desierto bajo un calor extremo. Mi cantimplora estaba casi vacía. La arena se metía entre los dedos de mis pies a pesar de las botas (a prueba de altas temperaturas) que había adquirido en una tienda especializada en deportes. El sombrero, empapado de sudor, apenas cumplía con su función. Las pestañas me pesaban. Iban cargadas de un patuque mezcla de los elementos de la naturaleza con los de mi cuerpo. No se veía ni una muestra de arbolito en el horizonte. Todo se veía igual, monótono. Mi compás me indicaba la ruta así que seguí confiando en él.

Una prueba más…, pensé. Una más de resistencia, de perseverancia, de voluntad.

Mi objetivo estaba claro. Miraba lo que parecía ser hacia delante. Cantaba las canciones de mi infancia con la poquita energía que me quedaba. Sabía que me quedaban algunos días hasta lograrlo.

De pronto, unas rocas a la distancia. Me dirigí poco a poco hacia ellas. El desvío era necesario.

Las rocas estaban dispuestas en forma de círculo casi perfecto. Recordé que no debía levantarlas por aquello de los escorpiones y serpientes que se protegen debajo de ellas. Me senté en una que se veía lo suficientemente "cómoda", dadas las circunstancias. Una botella verde oscura se apoyaba al lado de una piedra musgosa. ¡Qué extraño! ¿Musgo por aquí? Respiré profundo. Una suave brisa salió no sé de donde, como si me acariciara. La brisa empujó la botella hasta mis pies. No pude ignorarla.

La botella parecía haber viajado por el tiempo. Su etiqueta tenía sellos de diferentes países, de diferentes continentes. Interesante. Intrigante. Inesperada. La inspeccioné por todas partes. El corcho era de, Portugal, el vidrio de China. Era oscura y pesada para ser tan pequeña. La sacudí para saber si contenía algún líquido, pero no..., no tenía líquido. Sin embargo, tenía algo que no podía describir.

Saqué el corcho dándole vueltas con mis dientes. Cedió. La volteé. De ella salió una pelotica de papel, como las que nos tirábamos unos a otros en las clases aburridas. Al tomarla en mis manos se fue expandiendo. Olía rico, olía familiar. Era un manuscrito. Mis pestañas se aclararon. Mis manos, callosas por la vida, se suavizaron. La sed se calmó. No tenía hambre.

Comencé a leerlo. Las letras tenían voz. A medida que mis ojos se posaban en ellas, se avivaban y hablaban de forma clara y concisa. De manera muy sencilla tenía las respuestas a todas mis preguntas.

"Cada quien tiene la vida que le toca vivir. Cada quien toma decisiones que parecieran incomprensibles. Cada quien es dueño de su propio destino. Las circunstancias se presentaron porque las necesitabas para empujarte fuera de tu zona de confort. No te lamentes, no te arrepientas. Haz hecho lo que se esperaba de ti. Has sido valiente, has sido constante. Yo te acompañaré, como lo he hecho desde el día en que naciste. No tengas miedo y sigue. Hay cosas que no dependen de ti, que no puedes cambiar por más que quisieras. Libérate de esos sentimientos de impotencia, nadie te los agradecerá. Aún no has terminado tu camino. Algo hermoso espera por ti al final del desierto."

La botella se esfumó y yo seguí.

## *Antes De Terminar...*

Es de noche. Ya es hora de descansar. Pero no puedo irme todavía a la cama.

Siento como esa especie de remordimiento por no haber concluido mi día. Hay algo que aún me está faltando. Es así como cuando te vas de viaje y sientes que se te está quedando algo y no sabes qué es.

Me preparé una taza de leche tibia, como las viejitas de antes. Esta vez sin miel, porque estoy tratando de no ingerir azúcares. Es una de esas cosas que, a medida que uno va cumpliendo con el tiempo, debe dejar atrás. Ya no se necesita. En realidad, nunca se necesitó, pero ¡cómo se disfrutan los helados!

Ayer llovió y hoy amaneció haciendo frío, anunciando que, de verdad, el otoño ha comenzado. Aquí lo hace de a poquitos como para darnos tiempo de adaptarnos. En la tarde, aprovechando unos rayitos de sol que calentaron el ambiente, me fui a caminar.

De pronto, me paré ante unas hojas caídas que aún tenían remanentes de la lluvia; unas gotitas de agua, redonditas, sobre su superficie. Las contemplé y pensé en la realidad del otoño. Me sentí un poco como esas hojitas, medio secas, casi impermeables, comenzando a arrugarse, pero aun contribuyendo con los lindos colores de esta estación. Recogí una en mi mano. Me parecía verme en un espejo forestal. Pude ver en la parte posterior de esa hojita, las venas por las que un día su sabia se alborotaba de miedo y de alegría cuando se acercaba a ella algún insecto, algún parajito y a veces hasta algún venado para comérsela. Sobrevivió. Se escondía detrás del tronco principal y nunca la vieron.

Le di las gracias en silencio.

Seguí mi camino hacia la playa. Las olas del mar acariciaban las rocas que sobresalían en la superficie. El olor a salitre llenó mis pulmones y sentí que debía quedarme allí un rato, contemplando tanta belleza. De nuevo, miré hacia abajo, y una piedra verde, mojada por el agua salada, parecía como si brotara de la arena. La recogí, la contemplé, y pensé en todos los años que han debido pasar para que ella tuviese esa belleza tan especial. Es una belleza que cada piedra tiene. Son todas diferentes, de muchos colores y de muchas formas. Unas son redondas y lisas, otras alargadas y rugosas. Las hay para todos los gustos. Pequeñas, grandes, blancas, verdes, amarillas, negras, marrones…todas con alguna marca. Las han golpeado las olas, las ha rasguñado la arena. Han sobrevivido, como las hojas de los árboles.

Nosotros también hemos sobrevivido. Como las hojas de los árboles y como las rocas en la arena, somos todos diferentes, somos todos únicos, somos todos especiales.

Las otras hojitas del árbol se van cayendo poco a poco. Algunas sobrevivirán el otoño, y unas pocas el invierno, para dar paso a la nueva generación de hojitas. Lo mismo que nosotros. Se van nuestros padres y comienzan a irse nuestros amigos.

Las rocas volverán al mar, de donde salieron. Los niños que pasan las lanzan de nuevo al agua como diciendo que ese es su hogar.

Lo mismo que nosotros. Volveremos al universo.

Nos iremos algún día, en paz.

Ya me terminé mi taza con leche tibia. Estaba deliciosa.

Los ojos se me van cerrando.

Agradecida por este nuevo día, por cada nueva oportunidad. Soy parte del universo.

# *Don Yoyo*

Llevo horas sentada frente a la computadora, queriendo escribir, pero las teclas parecen esfumarse bajo mis dedos cuando trato de tocarlas. Las veo. Están cerca, y no las puedo alcanzar. Es una sensación extraña.

Me levanto de la silla y miro a mi alrededor.

La cabeza de da vueltas, o es el cuarto el que se está moviendo a mi alrededor, como si quisiera sacudirme, como si el silencio quisiera decirme muchas cosas.

Lo escucho.

Le pregunto…¿Dónde estás, que no te encuentro?

No me busques, aquí estoy.

La gata también está confundida, se sienta en mis piernas, me mira y maúlla.

Definitivamente algo está pasando.

Necesito escribir, pero no sé qué.

De pronto me ilumino como por arte de magia. Quiero contar, aunque sean cosas que parecieran no ser importantes. Y me llega esto…

Recuerdo un documental que me impresionó. La historia real de un muchacho tartamudo, morenito, poco agraciado, de familia pobre, de quien todos sus compañeros de clase se burlaban. No quiso y no pudo continuar sus estudios. Su padre, un alcohólico que se aparecía por la casa cuando se acordaba donde vivía. Su madre, maltratada y humillada frente a sus propios hijos que no sabían cómo defenderla. Se sentía deprimido. Podría haber escogido el camino fácil de las drogas para salir de su dolor. Sin embargo, un día se consiguió un yoyo en la basura y empezó a darle vueltas. Eso lo mantenía distraído, y cada vez, las vueltas del yoyo comenzaron a tener consistencia. El muchacho había descubierto su don especial, su regalo único. Comenzó a presentarse en las calles, en las plazas, en los centros comerciales. Bailaba al ritmo de su yoyo. Se inscribió en un concurso, y lo ganó. Su nombre apareció en las noticias. Con el premio del concurso, y el dinero que ganaba con sus presentaciones callejeras, montó una fábrica de yoyos. Pero él no estaba satisfecho, sabía que algo faltaba. Comenzó a atraer a otros muchachos que habían desviado sus caminos. Los invitó, los ayudó. Les enseñó el arte de dominar al yoyo. Les ofreció un camino diferente.

Esta semana lo tendremos invitado en la escuela donde doy clases.

Ya cuento los días que faltan para conocerlo. Por un momento siento que voy a conocer a una celebridad, y de cierta forma lo es. Su fortaleza de espíritu, su tenacidad, su dignidad y el respeto hacia consigo mismo ahora es ejemplo, es inspiración.

Todos tenemos algún don, pero ¿dónde está?

Está aquí, dentro de cada uno, está dentro de ti, y está dentro de mí.

Ahora lo reconozco, y lo dejo salir a través del teclado que tengo enfrente, y que se hizo visible para poderlo tocar. Cuando empujo las letras, que van saliendo casi sin pensarlo, escucho la música que produce cada una de ellas, cada una diferente, a su ritmo, y cuando las combino, entiendo. Ahora las veo plasmadas en el papel.

## *Cuando…Entonces*

Cuando la lluvia llora lágrimas de sangre,
cuando la música es el cacarear de tiros,
cuando la claridad del día se enturbia con humo,
cuando las esperanzas se ven amenazadas,
cuando ya no alcanza, o simplemente ya no hay,
Y cuando los oídos selectivos no quieren escuchar tu grito desesperado…

Entonces el eco de los llantos retumbará en sus pesadillas,
el humo les nublará la mente,
y la sangre indeleble de los caídos les manchará el alma.

Será el fruto de la semilla podrida de odio que regresará para envenenarlos,
será su propia avaricia que los carcomerá,
será su propia sangre que les reclamará.

# *Un Zueco de Madera*

Caminaba por el río, distraída, escuchando los pájaros cantar anunciando la primavera ya pronta a comenzar, cuando de pronto vi un zueco de madera flotar, acariciando la orilla, como queriendo detener su nado. Al acercarme me dijo: "El río hasta aquí me trajo. Estoy mareado con el vaivén del agua, del choque contra las rocas, y necesito descansar".

Me senté a escucharlo. Hablaba casi en susurros. No quería perturbarme con su ronca voz, carrasposa por haber estado en el agua por tanto tiempo.

Fue entonces que me contó su historia:

"Nací del álamo blanco, un árbol que muy buena madera dá. Un zapatero artesano, de esos que ya casi no se consiguen hoy en día, me tomó entre sus manos. Me miró, me acarició, y con cinceladas mientras escuchaba su música clásica que siempre lo inspiraba, comenzó nuestra creación. Sí, porque no me hizo a mí solito, no hubiera servido para mucho. Fuimos dos, como copias cuando te miras al espejo.

Nos llevó entonces al mercado campesino donde llamamos la atención de la esposa del pescadero, quien también vendía en el lugar lo que su marido traía a diario del mar. Nos compró y nos llevó a su casa donde por mucho tiempo caminamos sobre la tierra húmeda mientras ella, con su espíritu alegre, plantaba tulipanes y otras flores de muchos colores. Era un lugar hermosísimo.

Un día de otoño cayó una tormenta como nunca se había visto en ese caserío y con su fuerza inundó y destruyó lo que encontraba a su paso. Las cosechas se perdieron, y nosotros los zuecos, junto con muchos otros recuerdos, salimos flotando río abajo. No estábamos acostumbrados a tanto movimiento, y en un momento perdimos contacto. Tuve que seguir solo. Tragaba agua. No quería hundirme. Nunca supe lo que pasó con "mi otro", ya no recuerdo si soy el izquierdo o el derecho, y en estos momentos, ya ni eso importa. Sólo deseo sobrevivir, llegar a puerto firme".

Me recogiste, me escuchaste, me secaste, me cuidaste, me ofreciste un hogar. Hoy soy un adorno especial lleno de tierra, mirando por la ventana, esperando algún día volver a ver a mi otra mitad. En mí tengo sembrados dos bulbos de tulipanes que me recuerdan el hogar que tuve que dejar. Me tocó transformarme. Mi cambio ha sido profundo, no podré volver a caminar, pero siempre estaré agradecido por tu gran generosidad.

# *Una Bienvenida con Sabor*

El aroma del café viene volando como en las comiquitas, y debo levantarme para irlo a saborear. ¡Cuántos recuerdos me trae! ¿Un cafecito? Se escuchaba siempre cuando se visitaba a alguien, una bienvenida con sabor venezolano. Un negrito, un marroncito, colado, tetero, con leche...de cualquier forma era perfecto. Fue traído a nuestro país por los Jesuitas y se daba principalmente en la zona de Los Andes. Un día, en una época no muy lejana, llegamos a ser el tercer exportador mundial de tan rico producto.

Regreso a mi tacita para que no me cubra la nostalgia, y me pongo a pensar en los otros olores que me traen buenos recuerdos que quedaron grabados en algún lugar de mi cabeza. Cada vez que pienso en ellos es como si los oliera de nuevo, como si los tuviera presentes, y con ellos, la asociación de momentos muy especiales.

Así los interpreto:

| | |
|---|---|
| El olor a grama recién cortada | ....frescura |
| El olor a mar | ....energia |
| El olor a eucaliptus | ....aire puro |
| El olor a lluvia | ....limpieza |
| El olor a libros | ....sabiduría |
| El olor a talco de bebé | ....a mis hijos cuando eran pequeñitos |
| El olor a plátano frito | ....a mi comida criolla |

El olor a caballos ....estímulo
El olor a hallacas ....a navidad
El olor a rosas ....a mi mamá.

Puedo pensar en muchos otros, asociados en su mayoría a mi querida tierra natal, que algún día olerá de nuevo a libertad.

# *Lagrimas*

La hierba está todavía mojada por la lluvia que cayó hasta hace unos minutos. Un pájaro gris camina cuidadosamente sobre ella como si lo hiciera en puntillas, con varios palillos en su pico, sin hacer mucho ruido.

Es esa época del año donde seguramente el destino de las hierbas secas sea una chimenea abandonada, y que, al entretejerse, formarán un nido seguro para nuevas vidas, que mantendrán ocupados a sus padres mientras cuidan de los polluelos que aún no sepan volar.

Otros pajarillos compiten por el pan rallado que acabo de arrojar en el patio, disfrutando la fiesta del domingo ante mis ojos. ¿Será sólo mi imaginación, ó es ésta, en realidad, una alegre serenata audiovisual como su forma de expresar agradecimiento?

Esta madrugada es especial, y trae a mis pensamientos un enfoque casi filosófico. Me hace reflexionar sobre las grandes melodías irreemplazables de la naturaleza. Cuando pensaba que no había tiempo para ello, me conectaba a dispositivos electrónicos con un adaptador para los oídos, repitiendo la música que tarareaba con desafinados tonos. Ahora encuentro que la naturaleza prevalece, sus sonidos no necesitan ser modificados.

Sumergida en el goce, el tiempo pasa lentamente, y entonces, lo desconocido irrumpe y el miedo controla mi cuerpo. Comienzo a escuchar el sonido del silencio a mi alrededor. Es un lenguaje privado, único, y en un idioma que sólo soy yo capaz de descifrar, es mi lenguaje personal.

Anton Corbijn me viene a la mente: "Un hombre con todo en el mundo busca un lugar tranquilo para sentarse"...Sus palabras me hacen llorar y sentir, a la vez, lo muy afortunada que soy. El destino me ha traído aquí.

De repente tengo necesidad de buscar un taburete.

Mis lágrimas hoy son de alegría. Brotan como un sudor ocular emocional conectado directamente a mi pecho.

Otras lágrimas, conectadas con mi tiempo, son confusas. Me sirven para consolar viejos dolores, pérdidas que no pude evitar.

Los animales también lloran. Sus lágrimas son penas incontrolables, incomprensibles para sus almas que sólo viven en el presente.

Mi llanto purifica el alma, y entonces me encuentro de nuevo regocijándome al ver los pájaros comiendo su pan, piando sin cesar.

# *Barrotes*

Prisioneros afuera y adentro para salir y para entrar,
para permanecer o para cruzar.
Barrotes en las ventanas y en las puertas,
barrotes en las cárceles,
todos privan de libertad, de vida, de andar.
Los pasamos como animales de circo,
como tigres del zoológico, uno tras otro,
y seguimos viéndolos como las planas en los cuadernos,
siempre iguales, siempre infinitos.
El mundo está afuera de ellos, fuera de los barrotes,
Dáte vuelta, ármate de valor.
Atrévete y sal de tu encierro,
del que sólo tú tienes la llave,
del que sólo tú decides tus momentos.

# *Miedo*

Temer a lo que no existe,
temer al fracaso, temer al olvido.
El fracaso calculado por el temor es debilitante,
Pero es que realmente existe, o son las caídas y las levantadas
un triunfo en sí mismas?
El triunfo reflexionado por la ilusión es riesgo, pero es también riqueza espiritual.
La inseguridad bloquea las oportunidades, la confianza las atrae.
Cualquiera sea tu deseo, recogerás su fruto.
El tiempo es tu aliado y tu motor.
¿Y la vida?
Una caminata, un recorrido, un pasar, un regalo,
una bendición.

# *La Otra Vida de Maya*

El zumbido de las abejas revoloteando entre las flores es como oírlas cantar mientras llenan sus barriguitas con el néctar fabuloso que les ofrece la naturaleza. Siguen su vuelo, con la limitante de las responsabilidades propias de ser una abeja, cuidar y alimentar a su reinita, quien, a la vez, es su madre.

Maya, la abeja reina, tiene otra vida, una vida que ella sólo conoce, ya que es única. Salió a volar sólo una vez en su vida, y la siguieron unos zánganos. La mayoría morirán en sus intentos de fertilizar a la reina, otros sobrevivirán por algún tiempo hasta que las obreras los expulsen de las colmenas por no hacer sino comer y dormir, honrando su propio nombre.

Maya todo lo observa...y calla. Le cortaron las alas. Las palabras ´reales´ las tiene sólo ella, la que lleva la corona. No tiene con quién conversar. Las demás no pueden entenderla. Su vida, después del vuelo nupcial, se limita a poner huevos. También será testigo de la muerte de sus hijas, las obreras, ya que ella es la más longeva de la colmena.

La colmena vecina tiene una reina con alas. Liberada, puede salir a volar si así lo desea. No le cortaron las alas. Los sindicatos abejeros tienen una inteligencia colectiva y trabajan para el bien común, similar a las hormigas, en comunidades coordinadas.

Si me dejasen escoger mi vida, pareciera decir Maya, la abeja, volaría libre por el mundo. Pero el hombre decidió otro destino para mí. Me mutiló las alitas y ahora estoy en mi jaula de oro. Me sirven, pero no soy feliz. Veo otros pájaros en jaulas de oro como la mía, con las alas mutiladas para que no escapen, para que no vivan la vida para la que fueron creados. También veo seres humanos mutilados de muchas maneras, sin poder escoger su destino, sin poder salir de sus propias jaulas. Se han olvidado de la inteligencia colectiva, cada quien anda en su propio mundo.

...pero hay una gran diferencia con nosotras, las abejas. Las alas de los humanos son como las alas de los ángeles y pueden crecer de nuevo, fortalecidas, grandiosas. Si las extienden pueden volar tan alto como las águilas y seguir el ritmo de las estaciones. Los humanos tienen las llaves de sus jaulas. Las tienen en un bolsillo del que las sacarán cuando estén listos para volar. Mientras, seguirán sólo de observadores...y se les pasará la vida.

Mi último vuelo fue emocionante.

Las llaves que sonaban en mi bolsillo, abrieron mi jaula.

Ya no las necesito.

...y pasa un día más.

## *Sinfonía sin Escalas*

Las ramas de los árboles se mueven con fuerza, un lado a otro, al compás de un coro de que también va y viene, con altos y bajos, como si estuviera en un teatro y quisiera que todos lo escuchasen. Y tal como en un concierto de música clásica, hay momentos en que se enfurece y luego se calma. La sinfonía tiene nombre: "Sinfonía sin escalas", natural y espontánea. Parece haberse puesto de acuerdo con la época del año, el otoño, donde las hojas debilitadas caen como los papelillos en carnaval, dejando las ramas desnudas, esqueléticas, desprotegidas. Las hojas formarán una alfombra de múltiples colores; amarillos, anaranjados, rojos, verdes, con tonos de marrón, y cubrirán los caminos.

Los pájaros guardan silencio. Uno, y sólo uno, un arrendajo azul aventurero o perdido se para en la baranda y pareciera estar llamando a su compañera. Se acurruca, salta, vuelve. Se da cuenta que es mejor buscar un lugar seguro, y se va.

La gata se acerca a la puerta. Cuando se la abro decide que es mejor quedarse dentro de la casa. Yo también prefiero ser un poco más prudente hoy y pasaré mi día en casita. Me gusta. Disfruto de estos momentos en mi refugio personal.

La electricidad está amenazante. Se quiere ir, pero no está segura. Avisa.

Mejor busco unas velas y la linterna.

Más tarde, me acurrucaré como el arrendajo, y esperaré.